Praise

"*Late Blossoms* is an exquisite collection of short stories, moving the reader across time, country and space in the most magical and mystical of ways. The writing is poetic, just like its subject matter, and invites the reader to languish in the intriguing experiences of Jewish women creating art, no matter the obstacle. A mesmerising read."
ELISE ESTHER HEARST, AUTHOR OF ONE DAY WE'RE ALL GOING TO DIE

"In this evocative, originally structured collection of short fiction, Fima brings to life one of the most incredible cities on earth— Jerusalem of past and present—and the stories of women who contributed to the mythology of this place through their powerful artworks. This is an ambitious and enchanting book."
LEE KOFMAN, AUTHOR OF THE WRITER LAID BARE

"Merav Fima conjures the private reckonings of some of the country's most iconic painters and poets—the revered poets Rachel and Zelda, the storied painter Anna Ticho—as well as lesser-known but no less significant figures. A seamless melding of scholarship and invention."
JOAN LEEGANT, AUTHOR OF DISPLACED PERSONS

"Fima renders these visitors and immigrants to Mandate Palestine as real as the trees and flowers in Anna Ticho's garden, an amazing feat, leaving the reader hungry for more."
JUDY LEV, AUTHOR OF BETHLEHEM ROAD:
STORIES OF IMMIGRATION AND EXILE

"Impeccably researched, vividly described, and compellingly articulated, these stories serve as an evocation of place and also a tribute to the spirit of those who create their legacy through art. Fima has found inspiration in her own imaginary garden and peopled it with the soul of its inhabitants."
ZSOLT ALAPI, AUTHOR OF THE DANCE OF THE SEVEN DWARFS

About the Author

Merav Fima is a writer, translator, and literary scholar based in Melbourne, Australia. She holds a Ph.D. in Creative Writing from Monash University and her work has appeared in anthologies and literary journals worldwide, including: *Meanjin Quarterly*, *Parchment*, *Poetica Magazine*, and *The Australian Book Review*. She was awarded a grant for exceptionally talented writers, as well as for her translation of Gal Ventura's scholarly monograph, *Maternal Breast-Feeding and Its Substitutes in Nineteenth-Century French Art* (Brill, 2018). Several of her short stories have been honored in literary contests, and her forthcoming novel, *The Rose of Thirteen Petals and the Pomegranate Tree*, was shortlisted for the Wingate Award for Unpublished Manuscripts.

meravfima.com

Late Blossoms

stories

Merav Fima

www.vineleavespress.com

Cover design by Jessica Bell
Interior design by Amie McCracken

Author's own translation from the Hebrew of Rachel Bluwstein-Sela's poetry (in the public domain) from: *Rahel: The Poems* (Tel Aviv: Hakibbutz Hameuchad Publishing, 2003).

Author's own translation from the Hebrew of Zelda Schneurson-Mishkovsky's poetry from: *Zelda's Poems* (Tel Aviv: Hakibbutz Hameuchad Publishing, 2001).

Translations of Else Lasker-Schüler's poetry (in the public domain) from: Audri Durchslag and Jeanette Litman-Demeestere, trans., *Else Lasker-Schüler's Hebrew Ballads and Other Poems* (Philadelphia: The Jewish Publication Society of America, 1980).

Quotations of Nelly Sachs's poetry used with permission from Suhrkamp Verlag, Berlin. Poetry from: Nelly Sachs, Matthias Weichelt, *Werke. Kommentierte Ausgabe in vier Bänden*. 2010, Suhrkamp Verlag, Berlin. All rights reserved. Excerpt from *O The Chimneys* by Nelly Sachs translated by Ruth and Matthew Mead and Michael Hamburger. Translation copyright © 1967, renewed 1995 by Farrar, Straus & Giroux, Inc. Reprinted by permission of Farrar, Straus and Giroux.

Quotations from *Beauty and Love*, by Şeyh Galip, edited and translated by Victoria Rowe Holbrook, 2005. Used with permission from the Modern Language Association of America.

A catalogue record for this book is available from the National Library of Australia

For my mother and father, Lea and Dr. Joseph Fima, who instilled a love of books in me and continue to inspire me.

Table of Contents

Author's Note

In *A Room of One's Own*, Virginia Woolf writes that it would be interesting to imagine a meeting between the four great female English novelists of the nineteenth century: Jane Austen, Charlotte Brontë, Emily Brontë, and George Eliot. She states that the only thing they had in common is that not one of them bore a child. I, too, thought it would be fascinating to imagine just such a conversation between the great female writers, poets, and artists—all of them migrants—of Israel's founding generation, familiar as I am with the hardships associated with maintaining one's creative practice in a foreign land.

The first story sets the scene, demonstrating the effects of the establishment of the State of Israel in 1948 on members of different faith communities, and their continuing reverberation into the early twenty-first century. The following six stories are set at a literary salon, hosted at the Jerusalem residence of painter Anna Ticho and her husband, ophthalmologist Dr. Albert Ticho, in the mid-twentieth century. Each story features as its protagonist a different character, all of them women writers, poets, or painters of Jewish heritage, who had migrated from Europe. Inspired by historical figures, among them Anna Ticho, Rachel Bluwstein-Sela, Zelda

Schneurson-Mishkovsky, Else Lasker-Schüler, Leah Goldberg, and Nelly Sachs, these characters reappear in the linked short stories. Meeting on a regular basis to share their creative work and discuss the challenges of writing and painting in a new and unfamiliar environment, different language and culture, these women shaped the emerging State of Israel's literary, artistic, cultural, and intellectual scenes. Like their British predecessors, they had no children (with two tragic exceptions). The collection concludes with three contemporary stories, extending the legacy of these historical figures to fictional women engaged in Israel's current art scene.

Although the majority of the stories are based on my research into the lives and works of historical figures, I have taken poetic license in constructing the encounters between them, in order to explore their most profound emotions and experiences as women and as migrant artists. The stories also incorporate some of my own translations of their poetry, thereby introducing their work to English-speaking audiences.

Part I

Ein Kerem

1948, 2000

Bride Immaculate

She warned me that he would abandon me, that he would be as unfaithful to me as I had been to my vows, but I couldn't deny my heart's calling. And though he did leave me, it wasn't for the reasons she had envisioned. I know he would have stayed had he not been forced to flee.

But that was over half a century ago. The year was 1948. I was sent, aged twenty-seven, from my French hometown to the Holy Land; to live in a remote village amid the Judean Hills, reputed to be the birthplace of Saint John the Baptist. I was to join the Notre Dame de Sion congregation and help care for the ailing Sisters who were suffering from a severe outbreak of influenza—having been identified by the Mother Superior of my local abbey as being knowledgeable in herbs and natural remedies, a skill inherited from my Provençal mother.

That winter, the Jerusalem nights were bitter, and I found myself shivering as I lay in bed under a single woollen blanket, kept awake by the shrieking wind. I was unable to fall asleep even after repeating the rosary *ad nauseam*. When the sun broke through the clouds at midday, its warmth would caress me, and I yearned to throw myself into its beckoning arms. Lonely in the abbey, where I alone walked among the ill Sisters, and where all scheduled prayers and activities had come to a standstill, I ventured outside the iron gates to explore the adjacent hills, persuading myself that the abbey garden could not supply all of the plants needed to concoct the desired remedy, and therefore had no choice but to seek wild herbs beyond its crenellated stone walls. As Mother Superior was herself confined to bed with excruciating muscular pain and hallucinations and in dire need of my elixir, there was no one to question my prolonged absences or to forbid me from wandering to my heart's content.

It was on one of those sojourns to a terraced hillside, as far away from the abbey as I could reach, that I met him. I must have been drawn to the music soaring from his reed flute, stupefying the black sheep lying in a daze on the grass around him. I had, on previous occasions, spotted those same sheep skipping—wild with joy—from hill to hill, but the music sedated them like a tranquilizer, and they lolled on their backs in the sun. Identifying a tree trunk wide enough to conceal me from his sight, I removed my white apron, spread it over a patch of wild grass, lay down, and closed my eyes, allowing his music to take me on an enchanted journey to distant lands. I hadn't heard music (except for an organ and harpsichord accompanying the choral chanting of hymns) since devoting myself to God at the age of fourteen, and had certainly never heard music of this kind before—its exotic cadences sent a shiver down my spine, lulling me to sleep—a more profound sleep than I had enjoyed in all the weeks since arriving in Ein Kerem.

I awoke to find the man leaning over me. From my vantage point on the ground, his torso seemed to extend to the height of the pine trees. He smiled when he realized how startled I was; a smile that revealed a row of pearly white teeth glowing in contrast to his caramel-toned skin, a smile sincere with warmth and kindness. He extended his muscular arms to me—his hands rough on the outside but soft within—gently lifting me to my feet as though I were an injured lamb. Enthralled by his presence, thrilled by his touch, I suddenly noticed my apron still on the ground—stained green and brown from the damp grass—and bent over to retrieve it. He reached it first and, instead of handing it to me, let it drape over his forearm.

Placing a soothing hand on my back, he led me to a secluded spot under the luscious pomegranate tree, near an elusive brook, murmuring "*Habibti*," a word I could not understand. Any sound emitted by his deep, melodious voice, no matter its meaning, would have been pleasing to my ears. I longed to lean into him, to rest my head on his shoulder, and my lips somehow brushed his. I had never before felt a man's breath against my cheek, had never before felt so safe.

Only the chiming church bells recalled me from my reverie. I spun around and detached my body from his, pricking my exposed ankle on a thorn from the rosebush that had, until then, enfolded us in its exquisite fragrance.

—

I returned day after day and always found him lounging in the same spot, playing his hypnotic melody. Though thoroughly distracted by our daily encounters, I somehow managed to concoct the trusty lemon-honey-thyme syrup. One by one, the Sisters eventually returned to their duties and worship, and my free time was restricted. Mother Abbess, who had promoted me from Novice to the rank of Infirmerer in recognition of my contribution to the community's recovery, now gave me a sour look whenever she'd catch me daydreaming during her sermon, or a slap on the wrist if I doodled instead of transcribing the day's hymn.

After more than a month of poor concentration, she finally sent her deputy after me while I went out beyond the grounds one day. I will never forgive that spy of hers, forever depriving me of my one chance of true happiness, envious that her own prime had passed unfulfilled. If not for her, we could have continued enjoying our silent midday embraces, undisturbed.

——

The harsh winter had mellowed by the time Mother Abbess called me to her study a few weeks later. More and more flowers blossomed with each passing day, birds just back from their southern expedition cheerfully chirped, and the sun shone brighter. Almond trees adorned with fragrant flowers, like majestic brides, proclaimed the arrival of spring. We felt so secure amid their snow-white blossoms, forgetting that they could not camouflage us—he in his white *galabiya* and I in my starched black robe.

"Sit down, my child," Mother Abbess commanded when I stepped into her office with a curtsy. "Is there anything you would like to confess, Anne-Marie?" She examined me over the rim of her glasses, her green eyes magnified by the thick lenses.

Lowering my gaze, I muttered something about devoting more time lately to nature study than to the Holy Scriptures.

"By 'nature study' I take you to mean the exploration of bodily impulses and desires." I blanched; how could she possibly have discovered my most intimate secret?

She rose from her seat on the other side of the desk, strode across the room, and pressed a heavy palm into my shoulder.

"You have committed a most serious transgression in your lust for another human being, an infidelity toward our Heavenly Father. You must repent, make penance for your carnal sins, and retake your sacred vows; otherwise, you will have to leave the abbey and fend for yourself."

She walked me through the long, somber corridor to my cell—bare white walls with a wooden crucifix, the sole adornment, a narrow wrought-iron bed, a wooden desk and chair, and a porcelain wash basin. My only comfort was the window, framing the abbey's orchard, replete with olives, figs, pomegranates, and vines.

Tears rolled down my cheeks as I threw myself onto the stiff bed and heard the key turning in the lock; I did not know whether they were tears of longing for my beloved or tears of despair at the harshness of my fate and the difficulty of the situation in which I now found myself. Though I felt guilty for betraying Mother Abbess's trust, I could not believe that God would disapprove of a love as pure as ours.

I spent the next two weeks in a dazed sleep, interrupted only by the occasional gunshot, which I supposed to be a mark of celebration among the villagers. I only hoped that my beloved would clasp no other woman to his bosom during the celebratory dance, frustrated by my prolonged absence.

When Mother Abbess entered my cell bearing my daily portion of bread and water, I rose to face her for the first time in fifteen days. My feet barely held me, so weakened was I by my near starvation.

"I beg your pardon, Mother, but have no choice but to leave the Order and pursue my passion."

"It is, of course, your decision, my dear, but mark my words, he will abandon you and true happiness will continue to elude you if you step beyond our walls. I hope you have considered your options carefully." I kissed her outstretched hand, grabbed my woollen black cloak, and left the claustrophobic chamber with a curtsy.

—

I had lost all track of time, and everything beyond the monastery's crenellated stone walls seemed oddly dark and dreary, in sharp contrast to the lushness of the abbey garden and the fervent activity of the Sisters working the land. I did not look up as I crossed the garden, but from the corner of my eye, I saw one of the nuns flashing me a derisive smile. I knew at that moment that she had been the informant.

I was astonished at the stillness of the streets, usually so colorful and lively, with the joyful cries of children at play, and of bleating goats. The greater the distance I covered, the more the village appeared to be deserted. It was then I realized I hadn't even heard the *muezzin* for the past few days. This impression intensified when I reached the stone house with the blue door, where I knew my beloved lived.

The clothesline, always full of robes and linens hanging in the sun to dry, was completely bare, and the henhouse empty. The house stood silent. No flute music emerged from within, and no one sat drinking cardamom-spiced coffee while playing backgammon on the arched veranda. No one answered the door, even after repeated knocks, reaching a crescendo in their urgency. At first, I was relieved. What would I say to his mother or sisters if they found me standing there? How would I explain our relationship? Or even worse—what if his father, the Sheikh, opened the door, expecting one of his students for a tutorial? At least I would not look out of place, with the dark cloak thrown over my shoulders, complemented by a white headscarf. Perhaps I could claim that I had been invited to examine their livestock and administer a new vaccine against hoof-and-mouth disease?

I finally grew impatient and pushed the door open. The interior was as still as the exterior. Embroidered cushions were strewn on the floor, books and papers scattered all over the Persian carpet, and stained glasses stood on the low Damascene coffee table. There was no sign of humanity.

I collapsed onto one of the silk cushions embroidered with golden threads. Weeping in my loneliness and despair, I fell into a prolonged stupor. I awoke to the sound of soldiers yelling orders under the window. A pair in mismatched, badly fitting uniforms rapped the door with the butts of their guns, which they pointed at me when I had gathered enough strength to rise to my feet and answer the door. I raised my hands in total submission. After they had lowered their weapons, I somehow managed to comprehend from their hand gestures that all of the village's inhabitants had fled three days before—every house had been cleared overnight, their inhabitants rejoining their relatives in Jordan, Lebanon, or Syria—and the warriors had now come to take anyone who remained captive. It was then I realized that, just as Mother Abbess had predicted, my beloved really had abandoned me; not for the reasons she had envisioned (unless she had known about the evacuation and concealed the news from me), but abandoned me, nonetheless.

Recognizing that this land was the birthplace of all three Abrahamic religions, I tried explaining to the soldiers that

I had belonged, just a few hours before, to the nearby abbey and was of French Catholic origin, with no interest in the war and no desire to support or hinder either side. I then had the insight that would save my life: I told the soldiers about my expertise in natural remedies and my pharmaceutical skills and offered to establish a clinic in that very house, perhaps a branch of the Red Cross, to treat anyone wounded in battle. The soldiers surveyed the spacious house and nodded their approval.

The arrangement suited me, as it kept me occupied during the months in which fire was exchanged between Jews and Arabs. I was glad to remain in my beloved's home, hopeful that he would return at the end of the war and marry me, as a reward for my patience and unwavering devotion—finally granting me the happiness I yearned for.

While anticipating the arrival of my first patients, I prepared the house and put the rooms in order, immersing myself in family albums, imagining what our children would look like, and soaking the pillows on which he had slept with rose water infused with my own tears. I stroked his musical instruments, considering them too sacred to blow, and inhaled his distinct scent from the embroidered robes still hanging in the closet, worshipping the painted ceramic tiles on which he had stepped.

But he never did return. Several months later, Israel's independence was declared, and those same soldiers, now bearing badges of honor, returned to evict me from my beloved's former residence, claiming that the house was now needed to settle Jewish immigrants who had been expelled from Arab countries, and European Holocaust survivors. I had no choice but to return to France and lead a peaceful but solitary life in my hometown, tending to all those in need.

—

I have now returned for a final pilgrimage to the Holy Land, where I plan to live out my remaining days. Though I have given up all hope of ever seeing him again, I cannot help but wonder if he would recognize me, all bent and wrinkled as I am today. And though the Ein Kerem landscape has remained much the same, the houses appear dilapidated, and the blue paint on the door and windows of the Sheikh's home has started peeling away. Yet, despite the deterioration, it is now an exclusive neighborhood, long since annexed to Jerusalem's municipality, inhabited by artists in search of inspiration.

And that same spot where we first embraced—flourishing each year anew with the progeny of those original pomegranates, wild roses, and almond blossoms—has been discovered and appreciated by countless lovers since.

Part II

Ticho House, Jerusalem

1925–1967

Late Blossoms

It wasn't I who chose Jerusalem as the subject of my work;
rather, Jerusalem chose me.

—Anna Ticho

Anna ventured up the stairs to the attic for the first time since their move to Palestine, where she had, more than a decade earlier, followed and married her cousin, Dr. Albert Ticho, at the tender age of eighteen. In her left hand, she held a cotton canvas, on which she balanced a ceramic candleholder, watercolors, and a box of charcoal. Her right thumb and forefinger lifted the hem of her brown dress. She strained her eyes behind her thick oval lenses, handcrafted by her husband, which were gradually accumulating dust in snowflake formations. She struggled to see the sharp incline of the narrow stone steps in the darkness, and she ascended slowly, frequently stopping to adjust the sliding paint boxes and to catch her breath, careful neither to trip over nor tear her gown.

She tilted her head, concealing her nose behind the white collar of her blouse to protect herself from the dust. Her chin pointed to her brown leather boots, adorned with Swarovski crystals that glimmered with each step she took. She only wore those boots indoors, within the confines of her house, afraid to sully them in the dust and mud of the unpaved Jerusalem roads. Rubber boots and gingham dresses were the only materials suitable for outdoors, really, but there weren't too many occasions on which she left the house. She had everything she wanted, at home, and servants to fetch the things she needed.

Only inside the house, furnished with imported mahogany and heavily framed masterpieces, did she feel as though she still were in her Moravian hometown. Only there could she indulge in the same luxuries to which she had been accustomed in her privileged youth. The cultural and social elite of Jerusalem gathered in her home, as in a European salon, to discuss current artistic trends and dominant philosophical concepts. She was a well-respected hostess; her specialty *Sachertorte*, a perfect example of the traditional Austrian recipe, would be spoken of for days after being served.

She yearned to resume painting, as she had in Europe, but found no inspiration in the barren landscape. She admired her peers who created despite the emptiness. She was often moved to pick up a paintbrush, only to drop it again, leaving the canvas blank.

Nothing comes from nothing, she'd remind herself. *It is impossible to create a beautiful painting in this desolate city, surrounded by desert hills. There's nothing here to paint but muddy streets and slums, nothing at all inspirational. Painting should immortalize beauty; ugly things are never worthy of paint and canvas. Not to mention this direct sunlight distorts my perspective even of the things I most enjoyed painting in Europe.*

She'd thus avoid painting, though she preferred it even to baking. That day, she climbed up to the attic to find storage space for her painting supplies, tired of being constantly reminded of her lack of productivity each time she encountered them.

Her husband was at work in his ground-floor clinic, examining the last patient of the day, a dimpled woman with coarse black hair sticking out of her colorful, woven headscarf. Doctor Ticho always worked until the setting sun illuminated his office with soft rays of pink and yellow. As he no longer needed his wife to change sheets or to sterilize his instruments, she was free to wander, and explore their recently acquired home.

It was so large that she had not yet been to all its corners, though not as large as the family home in Europe. The garden, with its high stone walls, was her only refuge from the heat, noise, and dust of the desolate city in which they had settled. It was always shady and contained a greater variety of floral species than their European estate.

Anna made her way to the attic door and pushed it open with some difficulty, gaining momentum with each creak. When it finally opened, Anna felt her throat constricting. She coughed violently and covered her nose with her silk scarf, turning her face away from the entrance. Once her cough had subsided and the wave of dust plunged to the ground, she stepped inside.

She crouched and placed the loaded canvas down on the freezing, uneven stone floor. She then stretched her hands to unfasten the gown's velvet buttons, slowly manipulating them out of their loops with swollen fingers, numbed by the cold. Once she had undone the fifth and last button, she pulled her arms out of the sleeves and stepped out of the gown, afraid that it would become dusty. Dressed only in her long white undergarments, she took on the appearance of the ghost she imagined might inhabit the attic. If she encountered it over the course of her exploration, it would perhaps consider her kin and refrain from harming her. She tossed the gown aside with the heel of her boot, picked up the candle, and ventured further into the little chamber.

She stooped to avoid the low, slanted ceiling. Shining the candle on the walls, bare and moldy, she found nothing in the room but an old wooden dresser with a kidney-shaped mirror on top.

She approached the dresser, almost tripping over a stool, which she shoved into a corner. The candle's flame barely penetrated the thick layer of dust that had accumulated on the mirror over the years, struggling to find a clear spot to reflect its glimmer. Anna was glad she could not see herself in the mirror, as she was convinced that her hair must be gray with dust and that the loose white satin swelled her figure.

The dresser would be the perfect place for my painting supplies, she thought. *It is, in fact, the only space, unless I ask Albert to lug a chest up here; but he's always so busy and the staircase is so narrow. Besides, I wouldn't want him to find out that I've abandoned painting entirely. He's always encouraged me and will be disappointed if he knows I've given up. This will be my secret spot. Who would want to come up here anyway?*

Anna felt for a knob and pulled the top drawer open. It was heavier than she had anticipated. She heard something rattling inside. Reaching in, she felt a flat, cold, round piece of metal, as small as one of the buttons of her dress. She pulled it out.

"Amazing!" she exclaimed, her voice rebounding from wall to slanted ceiling. *We might be rich; there must be hundreds of coins in here. I could commission a new dress for myself and buy*

*Albert that antique Hanukkiyah from Charlotte's ... and perhaps
even plant more trees in the garden.*

She brought the coin to her eyes in an attempt to decipher
the bas-relief, but even under the direct light of the candle she
could not make out the inscription. The coin was covered in
rust. She picked up the canvas and boxes and collapsed on the
low, three-legged stool. She unfolded the edge of the canvas,
held the coin under it, and selected a soft stick of charcoal.

Barely seeing what her hand was doing, she rubbed the
charcoal over the canvas-covered coin to capture its imprint.
Black marks appeared on the grainy cotton canvas she had
stretched back in Vienna, where she had taken art lessons
before coming to Palestine, and her wrist began to ache with
the intensity of the motion. As her eyes adjusted, the candle's
meager light sufficed for Anna to make out a stylized seven-
branched candelabrum, framed by two curved branches with
pointed leaves and round fruits. She shivered, recognizing the
boughs of an olive tree, just like the one in the corner of her
garden. Perhaps it was that very olive tree that had inspired
the coin maker?

*An olive tree, here in Jerusalem? Two thousand years ago, the
last time sovereign Jewish symbols appeared on coins? Couldn't
I paint an olive tree, too? I've got my very own olive tree in the
garden, and a whole row of them lining Jaffa Road as it slopes
down to the Old City. In fact, I could paint a series of olive trees
in different lighting conditions, their leaves velvety in daylight
and silvery at twilight, like fireflies.*

*If the coin maker only engraved two branches, I could paint the
entire tree. If those branches were worthy of eternal preservation
in metal, so too is my olive tree at least worthy of canvas. I should
celebrate the richness of the landscape and its variegated colors,*

starting right here in my own garden. It cannot be any drier or emptier than it was two thousand years ago. Why look so far away for inspiration, when I've got such beautiful material, right here, in my backyard?

Anna threw the coin deep into her pocket and tucked the canvas and boxes of paint under her arm. Holding the candle in the other hand, she turned on her heel and hurried down the stairs, leaving the crumpled dress on the attic floor. Out of breath, she landed by the front door, pushed it open, and skipped into the garden.

At the same moment, another door swung open and the woman in the headscarf came out of the clinic. She stopped, just a few feet away from Anna, and stared at her. Anna realized that she was still in her white undergarments, but kept skipping toward the lawn. Murmuring something about immodesty and corruption of local mores, the woman turned and hastily walked away, slamming the gate behind her.

Tumbling down onto a damp spot at the roots of the rosebush, Anna called out to the mustached gardener to bring her a bowl of water to dilute the pigments. Surprised to see his mistress so underdressed and making such an unusual request, he dropped the hedge clippers and ran around to the back of the house to fulfill her desire at the manual pump. He did not return until he had related his discovery to the cook, who stuck her head out of the kitchen window, conveniently located right above the pump, overlooking the garden. Fond of gossip, especially about her own mistress, the cook did not let a minute pass before she divulged the news to the young maid, who had just returned from Mahane Yehuda market with a basket full of fresh vegetables for dinner.

Forgetting to thank the gardener, Anna grabbed the pewter bowl from his hands, unfazed by the drops that sprayed her camisole, too busy sorting her charcoals and spreading the canvas on her lap. Turning to avoid the setting sun, she found herself facing the imposing olive tree.

Picking up the same charcoal with which she had rubbed the impression of the ancient coin, and applying it to the same canvas, she began to delineate the bark. Her wrist shook and the lines seemed crooked. She struggled to add one branch and then another, before dressing the tree with leaves. As her taut wrist loosened, her eyes became more accustomed to the light seeping through the leaves. She began to see interesting angles between the two central boughs and in the curve of the trunk that she had not perceived before. She noticed details she had not known were there: the nest and sparrows perched on the branches and the stones, weeds, and insects at the roots. She discovered ripe olives at the foot of the tree, adorning it with an emerald necklace. Scooping as many olives as she could, she added them to the coin in her pocket.

Starting from the ground and working her way up, Anna drew from her position below the tree, until she reached the peak and filled the entire length of the canvas. The trunk rose like the torso of a slender, graceful ballerina mid-pirouette, pointing her toes and swinging her arms over her head.

Rearranging herself on the grass, Anna selected a slightly thicker piece of charcoal and retraced her initial lines, attempting to conceal their shakiness and expand the trunk's circumference. She chose a thicker pencil and shaded the wooden areas deprived of direct sunlight, imbuing them with volume. She used the thickest charcoal of all to add black eyes to the trunk and emphasize its veins.

She was about to open the box of watercolors and pick out the proper shade of green to fill in the leaves, matte on one side and metallic on the other, when a drop of water landed on the canvas and smudged the outline of the trunk. Anna looked up and saw that the sun had disappeared behind the clouds and the sky had grayed. Distressed, she attempted to absorb the moisture with the hem of her undershirt but succeeded only in further smudging the line. Collecting her colors and pencils, she hid the canvas under her camisole and ran into the house, unintentionally kicking the bowl on her way. The contents spilled, watering the rosebush.

Safely inside, Anna examined the canvas for damage but could not identify any. The smudge merely added to the impressionistic quality of her drawing. Satisfied, she signed her name on the bottom right corner of the canvas, dotting the final *vav*. Unaccustomed to forming the letters, she treated them as picture patterns instead. This was her first time signing in Hebrew on canvas. *Here I am, a Jewish artist, painting in the holiest of cities.*

Scraping her muddy boots, she scrutinized herself in the hall mirror. *Quite disrespectable in my undergarments,* she chided herself. *That woman was absolutely right.* She turned to examine her profile: her bun had come undone and oily auburn strands tickled the nape of her neck. As she unclipped her pin and attempted to fix her hair, she noticed a pale green stain right where her white undergarments had come into contact with the damp grass. She let go of her hair, clipping the barrette to the waist of her pants, and hurried to the bathroom, praying not to meet anyone on the way. For added safety, she held the canvas behind her back, covering the spot.

She encountered her husband, on his way to the kitchen after a long day's work in the clinic, where he had lingered an hour after his last patient's departure to arrange the files and disinfect the instruments. "Will you join me for coffee with whipped cream? All day I've been craving that hot *Apfel-strudel* you promised me." Noticing her hesitation, he asked, "Why are you dressed like that, my dear, and what are you hiding behind your back?"

"Oh, nothing ..." she stammered.

Albert attempted a peek behind her shoulders, but she spun, avoiding his glance. As he was blocking the passageway, she could not move on and finally acquiesced to his inquiries and gentle shove. She held the canvas up to him and dropped onto the floor, cross-legged, to conceal the stain.

He sat down next to her, took the canvas from her hands, adjusted his spectacles and contemplated the picture. "You're painting again, my dear, I'm so glad! What instigated this? It couldn't have been my coaxing."

"I found this coin in the attic," she said, fishing it from her pocket. "So I thought, if two thousand years ago olive trees were worthy of artistic depiction, maybe I, too, could paint our very own olive tree."

"Two thousand years?" he chuckled. "This cannot be more than fifty years old."

"But look at the date ... there are hundreds more where this came from. We might be rich."

"Don't be silly. You remember how greedy the previous owner was in our negotiations over the sale of the house. If those coins were worth anything, you can be certain that they would not have been left behind."

"Are you suggesting they're forgeries?"

"Not only suggesting, asserting. Wilhelm Moses Shapira, a former tenant, forged coins and ancient figurines. Besides, real copper doesn't rust, it only develops a green patina."

Anna dropped her hands and shook her head in disbelief. "All worthless, then?"

"Not worthless, my dear, if this is the product. If it has rekindled your creative spirit and inspired you to produce true art, it is worth every mil," he said, taking her hand in his and patting it.

She pulled her hand away. "If you'll excuse me now, doctor dear, I must dress for dinner. I'll meet you in an hour." She got up before he could ask any further questions. Keeping her back to the wall, she crossed the threshold and locked herself in the bathroom, leaving him seated on the corridor floor, examining the canvas and then the coin.

She considered calling her housekeeper, Farah, to help her, but was too embarrassed to show her the location of the stain. Filling the tub with lukewarm water, Anna disrobed and threw the satin into it. She rummaged in the cupboard for detergent and found an unscented soap-bar of pure olive oil. Stretching the drenched garments on the washboard, she vigorously scrubbed the stain. Though she normally disliked housework, or anything involving physical labor, she welcomed it this time. She even whistled a Moravian folk tune, accelerating her scrubbing motion to the rhythm of the song.

Anna examined her bare arms, so pale, rarely exposed to the Mediterranean sun. Her loose skin and untoned triceps vibrated as she scrubbed. *Could these be the hands of an artist, of a creator?* All this scrubbing was good for her painting muscles, which she had allowed to atrophy in their first years of residence in the Holy Land. The more she flexed her muscles, the more they itched to return outside and continue painting.

The stain finally disappeared. Anna wrung out the garments and laid them to dry on the windowsill. She then wrapped herself in the *schlafrock* hanging on the door, left the bathroom as discreetly as she could, and hurried to her bedroom to dress for dinner.

—

At 8:01 the next morning, Anna entered the ophthalmology clinic, tying the white medical apron around her waist. Raising his eyes from his desk, Doctor Ticho rose to greet her. Lightly placing one hand on her back, he kissed her cheek.

"Good morning, my darling. There's no need for you to work today. Go out into the garden and paint. It would be a much better use of your time. I don't have many patients today and have just finished preparing an advertisement for a clinical assistant, to release you from your nursing duties, so you may fully devote yourself to your painting. I'll join you outside in a little while. It's such a beautiful, sunny day; what a pity to spend it indoors." With that, he slid his hand down to her waist and untied the knot she had just made. Pulling the apron over her head, he folded it and put it on the back of a wicker chair.

Anna reached over to his desk and grabbed a bunch of blank papers. It was then that she noticed her charcoal drawing of the olive tree hanging in a thin metal frame on the wall behind the desk, under the shelf of Hanukkah lamps her husband collected. Her eyes met his and they both smiled as she left the clinic.

She retrieved her boxes of charcoal and watercolors from the bookshelf above the entrance hall mirror and opened the door, inhaling the fresh air, saturated with the fragrance of flowers. She followed the scent and selected a shady spot on the grass, next to the bougainvillea.

Anna dipped her paintbrush in water and swept it over the magenta compartment. Making a light brushstroke to warm up her wrist, gaining confidence, she started to reproduce the thin, almost translucent petals in different shades of fuchsia, gradually applying greater pressure to her paintbrush to achieve the desired effect. The flowers looked more like a bouquet, suspended mid-air, than wildflowers deeply rooted in her garden. She added their hooked black thorns, green stems, and white buds, as well as the blue flowers on whose territory they had encroached. When she was done, and about to soak the brush in water, her husband sat cross-legged on the grass next to her, admiring her painting.

He removed his vest, exposing red suspenders, unfastened his collar buttons and loosened his bowtie. "That's a very impressive juxtaposition of colors. It's amazing how the flowers as a whole look like a collection, but each petal is delineated as a separate unit. That's quite a significant feat, for one who hasn't held a paintbrush in so many years." He collected Anna's papers and pigments and held a hand out to her, pulling her up. Arm in arm, they strolled down the garden path toward the kitchen door, stopping from time to time to smell the roses, something they had never previously taken the time to do.

"Frau Doctor!" The cook's shrieking voice greeted them as soon as they entered the kitchen. "Look what I've done with the olives Farah found in the pocket of your petticoat." Anna blushed, her cheeks matching the bougainvillea, as the cook pointed to a glass jar filled with little green olives, slivers of garlic, slices of lemon and bay leaves, soaking in a clear liquid.

"Marinated them! They're good olives, they are. In three months' time we'll taste them. It's not an easy job changing the water and seasoning them, but I warrant they'll turn out good. Where'd you get them, ma'am?"

"In our very own backyard," replied Anna, pointing to the open window overlooking the garden.

—

After lunch, when the Doctor returned to his clinic to treat the afternoon's patients, Anna went outdoors to catch the last rays of sun. Walking the entire length of their garden, she stopped at the gate. Checking that she was properly attired and that her velvet hat was positioned correctly, Anna slid open the latch and ventured onto the street. She climbed the steep incline, taking smaller and smaller steps to avoid losing her breath, and stationed herself at the top of the road, where it met the Street of the Prophets.

From her elevated perspective, she could see the walled Old City with its domes and pointed towers. She began to paint the barren, hilly landscape, adorned here and there with bushes and thistles.

Anna sketched the hills in charcoal. Passersby stopped to observe her at work, but she did not allow them to distract her. She continued working as though they were not there, conscious of the few remaining daylight minutes. She was glad to finally draw a broad, expansive area, for which she had yearned ever since she'd moved from Europe. As the sun set, she vowed to return to that very spot the next day, to sketch the same landscape in brighter light.

—

Soon the garden became Anna's daytime atelier. She enjoyed sitting on the grass and spreading the materials of her art around her, no matter the season. Even in the winter rain, she saw new things to paint: sparkling drops of water and burgeoning green leaves. She celebrated the dryness of the summer, when she could experiment with different shades of brown and count the cracks in the parched ground.

She was eager to create new paintings with which to surprise her husband when he came out of the operating room to accompany her to lunch. She hoped to induce that unusual glimmer in his eyes, and the slight curvature of his lips. Whenever she presented a painting to him, she measured her success, not by his words, but by the approval that showed on his face.

Once, while absorbed in a painting of the gladioli at the rear edge of the garden, Albert approached her, earlier in the day than usual, accompanied by a man in a top hat. She rose to greet them.

"Anna, my dear, meet Professeur Edouard de Montpellier."

Anna wiped her paint-stained hand on her handkerchief and held it out to the man, who shook it eagerly. "It is a pleasure to make your acquaintance."

"Professeur de Montpellier is a curator at Galerie des Quatre Chemins," explained her husband. "He wishes to exhibit your painting of the bougainvillea that currently hangs in my office. Will you let him have it?"

Anna raised an eyebrow, surprised at the unexpected inquiry, and blushed with delight. *Paris, the world's art capital? My own little painting, created in two hours? Was it truly a work of art, worthy of a gallery? Was it truly more than a splash of color made to pass the time?*

"I couldn't keep my eyes on the vision chart, so drawn was I by your painting," said Professeur de Montpellier in his lyrical tone. "On the way over to you, we passed the bougainvillea bush. I was even more impressed by the beauty of your painting, its bright colors, and your spirited perspective. I believe the French people will cherish it and beg of you to let me have it."

Anna's heartbeat accelerated. She threw her husband a quick glance and was comforted by his smile and the sparkle of his eyes behind the spectacles. She was reluctant to have him part with her gift, but he seemed so pleased with the man's offer, so proud of his very own artist.

Anna acquiesced with a nod. The man gave her hand another vigorous shake and they headed back to the office to take the painting down from the wall, dismantle its frame, and roll it into a cardboard tube, for safe delivery overseas.

—

It was the Tichos' turn to host the company of German poets, painters, and scholars residing in Jerusalem. Anna greeted the guests at the garden gate, arrayed in her best emerald velvet dress and a hat adorned with a green peacock feather.

As she escorted Walter Reichart, the last of the guests, into the house, they passed the olive tree, bougainvillea, and gladioli she had painted over those last few months. Anna was pleased to see how beautiful they had grown; or had they always been thus, but she had never noticed?

The renowned sculptor remarked on the vividness of their color and the sweetness of their fragrance. He bent down to pick a budding flower and presented it to Anna with a shallow bow. "A blossom in exchange for a slice of your famous *Sachertorte*." Anna returned the courtesy with a light chuckle as she threaded the stem through her buttonhole.

They congregated in the vaulted salon where Albert had hung, especially for the occasion, the drawing of the olive tree, in the middle of Anna's series of barren hills. As the guests gathered by the eastern wall to examine the paintings, Anna balanced a platter of home-marinated green olives and offered them as an appetizer.

Doctor Ticho poured pure olive oil into the receptacles of the gold *Hanukkiyah* carved with a crowned roaring lion, a medieval French specimen gifted to him by Professeur de Montpellier. Striking a match, he lit the wick at the extreme left and recited the blessings. The flames illuminated the paintings from below, highlighting their shades and texture.

Picking up a silver pickle fork with an olive at its point, Reichart pointed a forefinger at Anna's drawing of the olive tree. "What a remarkable piece that is: so simple and yet so refined; so restrained and yet so passionate. To think that I must study the most obscure philosophies of Europe before I can even conceive of a distorted sculpture, while you seek and find inspiration in your very own garden. How come we have never seen your work before?"

Reichart raised the olive to his lips and chewed it with delight. Anna also inserted an olive into her mouth, letting her taste buds absorb the rich flavor.

Locked Garden

*In my garden I have planted you, / In the garden hidden—in my heart /
Rooting yourself in me.*

—Rachel Bluwstein-Sela

Rachel hesitated in front of the mirror hanging lopsidedly on
the door of the little shack she rented from Doctor Helena
Kagan, Jerusalem's favorite pediatrician. She lifted her hand
to readjust her straw hat, pulling back a stray strand of hair
that had fallen out of her dark bun. She was so tall that,
normally, her blue eyes could hardly glimpse the top of her
head in the mirror, but her shoulders had begun to slump,
and the mirror's edges now framed her pale face. She looked
down at her long cloak and skirt. Why so dark? Why always
black? *Well, no time to change now,* she thought, even though
all the German ladies would no doubt be adorned in frills and
finery. They would immediately guess she wasn't one of them,
even before she'd had a chance to utter a single word. Even
Doctor Kagan exchanged her white coat for elegant gowns at
these gatherings.

Rachel sometimes wondered why Doctor Kagan had invited
her. Though Rachel was held in high esteem as an accomplished poet who had made a name for herself, independently

of inherited wealth, she and the good doctor often disagreed. Everyone knew that tension between landlady and tenant could ruin even the closest of friendships, and they hadn't been friends to start with. Rachel was always surprised that, for someone reputed to have such compassion for the sick children of Jerusalem, Doctor Kagan barely showed her any, despite Rachel's ill health. In fact, she kept her distance from Rachel, afraid she would transmit germs to her patients, or so she said. She always struck Rachel as a tad arrogant, as though her scientific disposition rendered her superior. And, yet, though she was immersed in scientific research, she also valued art and music, and found her place at the Ticho salon not only as Albert's esteemed colleague, but also as a woman of culture and taste. Despite her apparent love of children, she too, remained childless.

Rachel had graciously accepted Doctor Kagan's invitation. Even though she had made a special effort to dress that evening, this was the best she could do. One hand already on the doorknob, she peeked into her purse, making sure she hadn't misplaced her notebook and pen—she was, after all, a woman on a mission. She had been sent by the new Hebrew newspaper, *Davar*, for which she wrote a weekly column, to report on the monthly salon held at the Tichos' house. Though it was situated just down the street, she'd never set foot inside, never been invited as a guest. Those Germans were endlessly protective of their culture.

Rachel stepped out into the courtyard and blinked until her eyes adjusted to the luminosity of the setting sun; she hardly ever left her bedchamber these days and wasn't used to the light, even this dim. She crossed the courtyard and nodded at her British neighbor, who was standing before an easel, palette and paintbrush in hand, examining the flourishing pear tree. *I wonder if he's noticed the initials* .ר.ז + .ר.ב. *carved into the bark, set inside a heart?*

Raising his head, he touched the rim of his hat in greeting, visibly agitated at being interrupted with so little daylight remaining. Rachel stole a sidelong glance at his canvas, still virtually empty, except for a few light brushstrokes. She looked longingly at his paint tubes. Painting had been her first love. If only she'd pursued this passion as she'd initially intended, she might not have been facing her own mortality at this very moment. She loved the smell and texture of the paints, but she'd abandoned her dream of attending art school in Europe after falling in love with the Land of Israel on her first visit as a tourist. The blueness of the sea (especially of Galilee), the brown, scented earth, the greenery of the fields she'd cultivated in Degania—these were more beautiful in her eyes than any brushstroke on canvas.

If only she'd returned to Europe after a short visit, and pursued her art education, the entire course of her life would have been different. All she could now paint with were words—and she still hadn't fully mastered the language; the editors of *Davar* were constantly correcting her mistakes, but they agreed to publish her poems and she was gaining a reputation as the national poetess. People had recently started stopping her on the streets to tell her how much they admired her work, even though the radius of her movements had been reduced to two or three kilometers from her shabby abode, where she lived in solitude—necessary to compose poetry, she told herself—in addition to the post office, where she'd present herself once a week to mail out her poems and articles to the newspaper. But the one person to whom her poems were secretly addressed, the one person whose opinion truly mattered, she never heard from.

Observing the painter at work, the words of a new poem came to mind, as though by inspiration:

Man awakes
And sees before his window
A blossoming pear tree.
Man cannot obstinately mourn
A single withered flower
When Spring presents him with
A huge bouquet at his window!

The verse resonated and carried her down the street as she made her way to the Tichos' house. She was intrigued to finally meet Anna, the renowned hostess, whose paintings of Jerusalem she admired. Perhaps she'd share some painting tips with her.

Rachel stalled at the gate to catch her breath. Her lungs were weakening by the day and even the brief downhill stroll from her shack to the Tichos' grand estate was trying. Opening the gate, she marveled at the beauty of the garden—concealed behind tall stone walls, she would never have imagined how lush it could be within. She tried to recall the names of the trees and flowers, though it had been over a decade since she had studied agronomy in Toulouse; her tongue rolled against her palate as she recited the Latin names: *Bougainvillea, Olea europaea, Ficus carica.*

An agronomist's work isn't all that different from a painter's, she thought—instead of a cotton or linen canvas, one's medium is the sacred earth of the Land of Israel. It's all about the arrangement of elements and shapes in order to achieve unity of tones, harmony of colors. Perhaps that's why she loved agricultural work so much. How she missed that lifestyle, the fresh air, and physical activity. Life in the city was exciting and offered more opportunities for socializing, but she missed the connection to the earth (*soon enough I'll be interred for all eternity*). This garden was the closest she'd seen in a long, long time to the fields of Degania, on the shores of Galilee, where she'd worked all those years ago.

Her poems were praised for the love of the land they conveyed, but did anyone know they were actually rooted in the love of a man? Both had remained elusive. Had she stayed in Degania and married him, would the mass of her poetry have been significantly depleted? Shouldn't poetry capture unfulfilled desires and fantasies? Had she continued to work the land she loved, would she have had the energy to stay up at night and compose poetry? Though her physical strength was now waning, her longing for Kinneret was so intense that it continued to propel her pen across the page.

Rachel knocked at the door. She could hear the rumble of lively conversation beyond, even before the door was thrown open by a maid dressed in a simple black frock overlaid with a white pinafore, who said: "Come in, you're late." She had lost track of time in her attempt to dress well, and then again in her contemplation of the loveliness of the garden.

Rachel followed the maid into the salon, where men and women in fine attire were listening to a man in a top hat discoursing about modern philosophy, citing Ludwig Wittgenstein's *Tractatus Logico-Philosophicus* as a prime example of the genre. She found the sophisticated German hard to follow. Though she spoke many languages, she had never quite mastered German.

Observing the enthralled faces all around her, she remembered how the home she had shared with her sisters Shoshana and Batsheva in Rehovot, when they first arrived in Palestine, had been the venue of many parties, dances, and social gatherings—though it was in no way as grand as the Tichos' house. She had always been at the center of society, until even her friends started ostracizing her, fearful of contracting her disease. She couldn't even dance anymore. Every twirl or pirouette rendered her breathless, too strenuous for her delicate figure, every exertion bringing her closer to her lungs' ultimate collapse. Dancing was another love she'd had to forego.

She envied Anna, who now stood at the heart of civilized society in Jerusalem. Rachel would have loved to be in her place, or at least co-hosting alongside her. It seemed to her as though Anna had fulfilled Rachel's own childhood ambitions; she was living the life she'd always dreamt of.

Rachel collapsed into an armchair in a corner of the room, catching her breath. She looked around at the elegant men and women in suits and lace blouses—scholars, physicians, and artists, by the look of it. The room was as ornate as its occupants—framed paintings on every wall, velvet armchairs, gold *hanukkiyot*, mahogany furniture. Her eyes were drawn to the artwork in the corner—Anna's painting of the gladioli—infusing the room with bright, vivid color. How it reminded her of the flowers she had cultivated at Degania, and of the innocent brushstrokes she used to paint in her carefree Russian childhood.

One after the other, the guests rose to their feet, deliberating one notion or another in rapid German. Rachel could only loosely follow, but jotted down cursory notes in her notebook, capturing a lively impression of the gathering.

At Anna's signal, Rachel rose to her feet and recited her latest poem, but quickly sat back down again, too exhausted to notice the other guests' reactions.

It was only when they reached the subject of contemporary German poetry and painting that they finally captivated Rachel's full attention. She was always looking for poetic models she could emulate in her own work, but hadn't yet found a suitable candidate in the entire Hebrew language, what with its patriarchal, religious overtones; so she had undertaken a profound study of the Russian women poets, particularly Anna Akhmatova, in an attempt to come up with a style better suited to a secular woman writing in the twentieth century. She'd spent much time translating poetry from Hebrew to Russian and from Russian to Hebrew. Though some may have considered it a waste of her talents, taking time away from her original composition, these translations were her teachers, that's how she had learned to write poetry in the first place. She abhorred the obtuseness of most contemporary poets, their convoluted style, seeking instead to express her complex thoughts using the simplest vocabulary.

Her ears perked up when a deep male voice mentioned the name Else Lasker-Schüler, apparently quite a sensation in the cafés of Berlin, and also a vibrant visual artist. "Who's to say she must choose between poetry and painting, or that the two are mutually exclusive?" The orator went on to say that Else was becoming known for her avant-garde Expressionist style and her overt identification in her poems with biblical figures, going so far as to dub herself Prince Jussuf.

Well, isn't that a novel idea? thought Rachel. *I've always thought of writing a poem about Rachel the Matriarch, lamenting her barrenness. That's the one thing I share with my namesake.*

Why is it that those of us who love children are deprived of bearing our own, while those who don't want them or may not be as affectionate—to them childbearing comes so easily? For aren't children supposed to be fruits of love? Was I denied children because I never found the love I sought? A soft cough escaped from Rachel's tightly drawn lips, as her lungs contracted around her aching heart.

As the speaker moved on to discuss the political situation in Europe, Rachel continued to ruminate: *It was my love of children that ultimately led to my demise. If I hadn't loved them so much, I wouldn't have sought work in a Russian orphanage and contracted the dreadful disease that now consumes me. It is not for naught that tuberculosis is known as consumption. I loved the children I looked after at Degania and was heartbroken to leave them, but was forced to leave the kibbutz once my illness was discovered.* Rachel could no longer suppress the coughing wave rising into her chest. She had hoped the warmer Mediterranean climate would improve her condition, but the effects of that brutal Russian winter never waned.

Perhaps I am withering away because I never fulfilled my maternal potential. Now that my body is past childbearing, is it destroying itself because it hasn't realized its most fundamental role? Another cough erupted, and another, growing louder, more persistent. *My poems will be my children; they will be my legacy, will not betray me, and will ensure that I am remembered long after my death. All I can do in the meantime is pour out my longing into words.*

Rachel tried to keep her mouth tightly shut, but a loud cough rose to her chest and escaped from her lips. She took a handkerchief out of her jacket pocket and raised it to her lips, but it was too late. She had already drawn the attention of her neighbor, who inched away from her, averting his gaze. When her cough grew louder, uncontrollable, he glared, getting up from his chair. "Would you mind stepping outside? You're quite disruptive, I can't focus on the lecture." *I am not wanted anywhere*, thought Rachel.

Only one face beamed at her—a schoolgirl in pigtails—clearly unaware of Rachel's threat to public health.

Resigning herself to her fate, Rachel began to collect her belongings when she discovered Anna in the vacated seat next to hers. "I'm so sorry, my dear, but I must ask you to leave; the other guests don't feel safe in your presence. I'd love to continue the conversation, if you don't mind waiting in the parlor."

"Excuse me," exclaimed Rachel as she rose to her feet and made her way out of the salon through the arched doorway, covering her mouth with her handkerchief.

To her surprise, she was met by Anna beyond the threshold. "I'm awfully sorry, but we really cannot have someone with a pulmonary disease among us. As you know, my husband runs a clinic from this house, and we wouldn't want to infect Jerusalem's most vulnerable. I wish I could invite you to regularly join our salon; I've read your poems in *Davar*, they're quite extraordinary, and loved the one you just shared with us."

Rachel nodded in acknowledgment of the praise, as Anna continued: "How about I come and visit you once a month, and fill you in on all that's been said and done here? I understand you're not too far away ..."

"No, not far at all, just up the street, though it feels like miles away."

"Wonderful, I often go up there to paint. It offers me a great vantage point of the Old City."

"I'll look forward to seeing you, then," responded Rachel, tucking her pen and notebook into her purse. "I think I've got all the material I need to write my article."

"Wait." Anna blocked her mid-stride. "Wouldn't you like a tour of the house? I'd love to show you my paintings once all the guests have gone. In the meantime, can I bring you some tea?"

Rachel nodded, eager for a hot drink to warm her heaving chest.

"Wait here and make yourself comfortable." Anna showed her into a separate sitting room in a vaulted stone enclave just below the entrance.

A few minutes later, a maid entered the chamber bearing a silver platter with a single porcelain mug and a plate laden with a thick slice of *Apfelstrudel*.

—

Inhaling the steam rising from the teacup, Rachel allowed it to warm her aching lungs and alleviate the pain. She sipped slowly, savoring the lemony balm.

She heard voices overhead, steps approaching the doorway, Anna's and Albert's voices saying goodbye to the distinguished guests as they prepared to leave. She knew that Anna would soon return.

To keep herself occupied, Rachel examined the paintings in the narrow sitting room. Her entire living quarters could easily fit into this one room. She pitied herself, that her life had become so dull, confined to such a narrow space, her movements so limited.

The paintings on the wall gradually grew more colorful—beginning with monochromatic charcoal sketches of an olive tree, followed by a silhouette of the Old City of Jerusalem, ending with brightly rendered floral arrangements at different times of day.

Just then, heavy steps came down the stairs and Anna, a picture of good health, her round, cheerful face bright, and her voluptuousness in clear contrast to Rachel's emaciated figure and translucent skin, greeted her. Anna kept her distance from Rachel, taking a step back every time she moved forward, as though they were engaged in a continuous dance, guided by invisible marionette strings, or as though they were pieces on a chess board, each moving in response to the other player.

"As I said, Rachel dear, I've enjoyed your poems in *Davar* and wish we could host you as part of our salon, but it would be perilous, you understand."

"No one's wanted me around since my illness erupted."

"I'd be happy to come over from time to time and fill you in on our monthly meetings. Do you have any questions about what you saw here today?"

"What gave you the idea to start this salon in the first place?" Rachel inquired.

Anna cleared her throat as she considered her response. "I did it for social reasons. It took me years to start painting again after we moved here; the move was quite startling, you see. Many of our friends followed us to Jerusalem, so I started hosting these gatherings to make them feel more at home, and to continue having some cultural influence, though I was no longer painting, dedicating myself to nursing instead. Soon their discussions inspired me to pick up my paintbrush again, while my baking satiated their stomachs," she chuckled.

Anna led Rachel up the stairs, through the various rooms of the mansion, each room separated from the next by a solid stone arch.

"Everything's so beautiful and I love the artwork on the walls, but where's the kids' room?" inquired Rachel.

Anna averted her gaze, a shadow crossing her face.

"You bring up a sore subject. We don't have any children. Albert and I tried for many years but in time, reconciled ourselves to the knowledge that we would never become parents, after our firstborn died in infancy and I experienced half a dozen miscarriages. I turned all my attention to my art. Albert's love sustains me, as much as, or perhaps more so, than any child's. I wouldn't have had as much time to invest in my art, nor in entertaining, had I been a mother." Anna and Albert seemed to be so deeply in love, reflected Rachel, and yet they had not been blessed either.

She'd always longed for children and loved the ones she had cared for at Degania. Why hadn't she earned the love of the man she'd yearned for? Why was she destined to remain nothing but a muse, inspiring him from afar, while his hand was bound to another?

She's got a gold ring on her finger
But my iron cables—are strong
Sevenfold!

Why had that other Rachel been chosen to bear his seed?

Deep in thought, the two women were almost at the front door again, the tour of the house over, when a loud knock sounded. A maid rushed to answer the door, her pinafore rustling.

A small, dark figure appeared, the darkness of her skin evident from the glimmers cast by the setting sun. Her slight stature surprised Rachel, given the strength and persistence of her knock.

Anna's jovial face instantly changed, her eyebrows joining at a sharp angle, her usually cheerful mouth downturned.

The dark-skinned woman carried a baby close to her bosom; wrapped in a long floral shawl, she nursed from her exposed breast. Over her shoulder, she held a silvery velvet gown, which she presented to the mistress of the house. Rachel followed a few steps behind Anna. Even from a distance, she could glimpse the sheen of the gown, the intricate gold-thread embroidery woven with shimmering beads. She'd never seen that kind of embroidery before.

"Why are you late?" asked Anna, her voice stern. "I'd intended to wear it to today's meeting, which ended over an hour ago. Instead, I had to embarrass myself before my guests by wearing the same gown I wore last month." Her thumb and forefinger pinched the edge of her skirt, fanning it out to indicate the source of her embarrassment. Rachel stared at it, puzzled. It looked so elegant, far superior to anything she owned or could ever hope to wear.

"I'm sorry, ma'am," she said, in a small voice, emerging from her dark lips. "My two-year-old twins were sick with fever, and this baby kept me up all night nursing, so I wasn't able to complete the commission on time. I have nine children at home, ma'am. I can assure you I did my very best."

Rachel watched as Anna's face gradually softened. "Come in, sit down," she offered. "Get her a cup of tea," she ordered the maid.

"You should take your twins to see Doctor Kagan at Tipat Halav," advised Anna. "She's a real angel." In an instant, Anna was gone, leaving the woman alone with Rachel.

Rachel struggled to keep her hands to herself, rising, as though by compulsion, to caress the infant's delicate features, his soft dark curls.

If only I had a little son,
To grasp his hand and slowly walk him
Through the garden paths.
Embittered like Rachel the Matriarch
I await
Him.

The verses formed in Rachel's feverish mind.

She diverted her hand so she wouldn't infect him, and instead, caressed the soft velvet of the gown the woman had brought, holding the collar close to her eyes so she could examine the delicate embroidery more closely.

"This is meticulous work; I've never seen anything like it."

"Thank you, ma'am, it's a traditional Yemeni pattern."

"Where can I purchase one of your designs?" inquired Rachel.

"I work for the Bezalel workshop," she responded.

"You could start a fashion line of your own," said Rachel. "I'm sure you'd be very successful."

"You're too kind," responded the woman.

At that moment, Anna re-entered the room carrying her box of charcoal and a stack of paper.

"Would you mind if I sketched you and your baby?"

"Not at all. Go ahead, so long as you can do it with me seated; it'll give me a few minutes' rest."

Watching her carrying the child, Rachel felt tired, her body weak. "I'd better get going then. I've got all the material I need to write my column."

Anna barely nodded goodbye, so absorbed was she in her drawing, her charcoal stick already sketching a quick outline of the woman and her baby.

As Rachel was about to exit the mansion, the girl in pigtails intercepted her and asked if she would read some of her verses. Rachel let her down gently. *I barely have the strength to hold the weekly newspaper, but I imagine she'll succeed, she looks like a determined young lass.*

Rachel made her way back up the steep hill to the Street of the Prophets, pausing every few steps to catch her breath.

When she entered her home, she removed her hat and sat down at her desk. She quickly transcribed her notes and jotted down her impressions of the Tichos' salon, making sure to mention the woman who had delivered the dress at the end of the evening. Perhaps her column would serve as advertising for her garments, and would help her out in some small way.

The article complete, Rachel stuffed it into an envelope, along with the poem she had composed that morning about the pear tree flourishing in the courtyard, addressed it to the editor of *Davar* and licked the envelope, thinking of all the germs swarming in her saliva.

She planned to deliver the envelope to the post office right away but was too tired to leave the house again, so she undressed and got into bed.

—

Anticipating Anna's arrival the following month, Rachel wondered if she was already walking up to the Street of the Prophets; had she already reached the courtyard? Would she be struck by the majestic pear tree, notice the initials carved into its trunk?

Anna arrived even earlier than she'd expected, and Rachel was startled by her knock. Paralyzed in her bed, both from lethargy and her reluctance to admit Anna into her modest abode, she heard Anna knocking again, harder this time. "Rachel," she called, "I know you're in there, open up!"

Rachel finally responded in a weak voice: "Come in," followed by a barrage of coughing.

Turning the doorknob, Anna entered. Daylight blazed into the property on the edge of Doctor Kagan's estate. Rachel squinted, noticing the cloud of dust adorning her guest's petticoats and long skirt. She must have been sweeping dirt off the unpaved road.

Wiping sweat from her brow, Anna searched for a chair. Finding none, she settled on a low stool, which she moved nearer to the bed.

"You'll never guess who made a surprise appearance at our salon two days ago," said Anna, sitting down.

Rachel turned her head, curious.

"Zalman Shazar, just back from Europe on a brief visit. He brought some poems to share with the assembly, all of them clearly inspired by your latest poems in *Davar*."

Rachel opened her mouth to respond, but all that came out at first was an inaudible gasp.

"Don't despair, Rachel; science has made great strides in the cure of pulmonary disease."

"I can't believe he was so close and didn't come to see me," whispered Rachel.

"He must have been in a hurry."

"Am I forever destined to be nothing but a man's muse?" she lamented.

The burden of your silence oppresses my vitality
The sword of your silence slays my heart
I await
The blood of my poem reddens around me.
I am still here
Strike me with your words! I beg you—do not remain silent!

Why couldn't I be loved and respected as an equal, as a partner? thought Rachel. *And why was I destined to be both muse and creator, with no one to inspire my own poetry?*

Why could some men use her for their own artistic inspiration, while refusing to reciprocate, unable to bestow upon her the love for which she yearned? Or was she to blame for ignoring him all those years ago, among the boating party at Kinneret, not returning his bashful smile as they set sail among the company of pioneers?

"Sit up, Rachel," said Anna, "I've brought you some *Mandel-brot.*"

"I can barely raise my head from the pillow, I've grown so weak. So many ideas that crossed my mind have slipped away; I wasn't even strong enough to put pen to paper."

"Nonetheless, sit up, the *Mandelbrot* will strengthen you," said Anna, supporting Rachel's head to help her lift her torso, and bringing a slice of the crunchy biscuit to her lips. Rachel chewed slowly, savoring the rich taste.

She was starting to wonder—who was the locked garden? She'd once written a poem asking:

Who are you? Why does an outstretched hand
Not meet a sisterly hand?
A locked garden. No path to it, no way.
A locked garden—man.

But was it really Zalman who was the locked garden or was it actually her? Had she allowed the rose he had given her that day at the Sea of Galilee to implant itself inside her heart, to grow roots and thorns, the red petals slowly dropping one by one from the stem, until nothing but thorns remained?

"Did he even ask about me?" she inquired.

"Yes, I told him you'd attended last month's meeting, but that you're now too sick to join us."

"Didn't he ask for my address? Wasn't he interested in seeing me one last time?" Rachel had secretly held on to the hope that he'd come and see her when he heard of her illness; she believed that the sight of him would serve as an elixir for her damaged lungs.

"I told him you live just up the street. I even offered to accompany him here, but he said he must catch a boat back to Europe, departing from Jaffa the very next day, and could not linger in Jerusalem."

If only she'd been welcome at the Ticho salon, she would have met him there. Rachel imagined the unlikely encounter—how she would have blushed or gone pale at the sight of him, as he entered the door and crossed the threshold, so tall and handsome, dressed in the latest European fashion, wearing a dark suit and a top hat. At first, she would have thought that she was hallucinating, that the ailment of her lungs was now affecting her mind, but then he would have walked right up to her in a determined stride, and, the closer he got, the more real it would feel, until he stood at arm's reach, examining her faded beauty, placing one hand on her shoulder, another around her waist, pulling her close to him, planting a kiss on her cheek. "Rachel! My dear! It's been so long," he would exclaim.

But she wasn't welcome at the salon, or any gathering, and her only companions were her verses. When she couldn't fall asleep at night, she'd recite the words of her poems she had memorized to dispel the darkness.

In my great loneliness
I lie silent for hours on end.
The submissive heart forgives.
If these be my last days—
Let them be peaceful.

The cadence of the verses soothed her; their beauty comforted her.

"Anna, my dear, will you kindly look on my bedside table, there's an envelope there."

Anna got up and rummaged through the scraps of paper on which Rachel had scribbled notes, fragments, and poetic passages. She found the envelope.

"Could you deliver it to the post office for me? It would be a great act of kindness."

"Yes, of course, Rachel, it would be my pleasure."

"Thank you, that's very kind of you. The envelope contains what is, no doubt, my last poem. I do not know if I'll ever have the strength to write another. The muse doesn't visit those who don't have the strength to contain it, and I'm too tired of being both another man's muse and my own. I'd normally have written ten poems in the time it took me to write just this one, but it will, at least, be my legacy for eternity. Have compassion for me, since Zalman certainly won't."

"Goodbye, Rachel," said Anna, squeezing her hand before rising to her feet and sticking the envelope in her purse as she closed the door behind her.

Enchanted Bird

Every rose is an island / of eternal peace.
—Zelda Schneurson-Mishkovsky

Zelda sat at her desk wearing her pleated school uniform. The navy blue and yellow check was not pleasing to the eye— *so jarring*, she thought. She'd once heard that the colors had been chosen to remind the schoolgirls of the majesty of the Divine, and of the modesty expected of them when standing before the Eternal Throne. To Zelda, it just felt dull.

Until one day, in class, when they studied Ezekiel's vision of the Throne of Glory. After that, she could no longer look up at the sky, or anything blue for that matter, without envisioning the sapphire stone that stands at the base of the Holy One's throne.

Though she loved the poetic language and imagery of the prophets, she found her teacher hopelessly boring, her monotone ruining the lyricism of the biblical verses. Her gaze drifted off as she looked out the window, skipping from tree to tree to blue patch of sky just outside the classroom window. Her eyes fixated on a small, blue-chested bird—*a hummingbird?*—that had just landed on one of the branches of the pomegranate tree. Now it dived down, beak first, eagerly consuming the nectar of the roses growing along the school-house's outer wall.

In every rose lives
A sapphire bird, Zelda thought to herself.

Zelda only half-listened to her teacher's drone. Grasping a blue ballpoint pen, her hand glided across the page, doodling instead of copying the biblical passage inscribed in white chalk on the blackboard at the front of the classroom. The tip of her pen slid across the ruled lines. Slowly hatching the blue marks, a curved head appeared at the top of the page, followed by a beak and feet. Doubling and tripling the lines and endowing them with volume, the marks grew darker, more intense.

A blue bird materialized on the page in front of her just as she became aware of her teacher's voice angrily repeating her name: "Zelda, wake up. Princess Zelda!"

She looked up at the teacher's face, furious that her pupil was inattentive, that she didn't answer when called upon.

"I'm sorry, Mrs. Silverstein, I didn't hear the question."

Mrs. Silverstein walked down the aisle with a resolute step.

"No wonder you couldn't hear my question. Let me see what's been distracting you."

Extending her hand, she snatched Zelda's drawing from her desk.

"Please stay behind after the bell rings."

Zelda could feel her face burning. She instinctively raised her hands to cover her crimson cheeks.

As the teacher continued, Zelda buried her face in her sacred book and didn't look up from her desk, even when she heard the bell ringing and the shuffling of the other girls' shoes against the *balatot* of the slate floor.

When everything had grown quiet again, she could smell her teacher's distinctive scent as she approached—the cheap perfume favored by the matriarchs of Jerusalem, a replica of an expensive Parisian brand, no doubt. From that day onward, she would grow nauseated whenever she caught a whiff of that scent.

"Zelda, sit up straight," commanded the sharp voice.

Zelda raised her head from her book and straightened her back.

"Zelda, I've noticed you've taken an interest in drawing lately."

"Yes, ma'am," she stammered.

"You clearly have some skill, some raw talent, Zelda, but are you aware that by drawing during Bible class you are making the sacred profane and blaspheming?"

Zelda blanched, her face growing pale.

"Have you forgotten the Second Commandment?" continued Mrs. Silverstein.

"No, I haven't."

"Could you recite it for me?"

Zelda closed her eyes. *"Thou shall not make any graven image."*

"Precisely. Your drawings of birds and other living creatures are nothing but heresy."

Heresy? Zelda's entire body shook. She had not meant it as an insult to the Divine. On the contrary, she felt that, by capturing an impression of living beings on paper, she was glorifying God's creation.

"Never forget, Zelda, you are a scion of a formidable Hasidic dynasty, a descendent of the great Lubavitcher rebbe. Do not bring dishonor upon your family with this ridiculous hobby of yours."

Head lowered, Zelda paced the length of the classroom and left the schoolhouse. It was true that she'd always dreamt of becoming an artist, even harbored secret hopes of completing her artistic education in Europe, copying the works of the Old Masters. But what if she did bring shame to her family? What if painting wasn't an appropriate pursuit for a pious girl?

Perhaps she should leave the seminary and enroll at the Bezalel School of Arts and Crafts. Although she knew she would never fit in there. Bezalel was for secular men and women, who smoked cigarettes and danced cheek-to-cheek at Café Atara. She would feel completely out of place.

She made her way toward the small apartment she shared with her mother in a cramped building in Kerem Avraham. What would her sickly mother, who hardly ever got out of bed, think if she decided to study drawing and painting, in addition to her household chores? She'd always encouraged her to pursue her dreams, but when the moment actually came, would she agree to release her from her household duties for just one hour each day, in order to pursue a frivolous ambition, sure to bring shame upon the family? Her mother's wishes for her were withering away her spirit. She paused in the courtyard outside her building and prayed to God for clarity.

She was confused, and didn't know how to proceed, but one thing she knew for certain: if she ever became a teacher, she'd like to be the kind who inspired her students to pursue their dreams and encouraged them to realize their ambitions, not one who shamed and discouraged them like Mrs. Silverstein. She hoped to be the kind of teacher who would allow her pupils to discover the divine sparks within themselves and in their peers.

Zelda took a deep breath and climbed the steep staircase to the dark, dingy apartment. As usual, her mother was still in bed, under the patchwork quilt, and the curtains were still drawn, preventing the bright sunlight from penetrating the window and illuminating their modest abode, even though it was already two o'clock in the afternoon.

Zelda struck a match and ignited the gas burner to warm the borscht she'd cooked early that morning before leaving for school, her hands still stained purple from peeling the beetroots.

She observed the flames emerging from the gas spout. The yellow, orange, and red tongues of fire reminded her of the majesty of God. As the temperature rose, the blueness at the heart of the flame evoked the sapphire stone; God's heavenly throne.

She couldn't bear to be the one to bring shame upon the family's good name.

Lifting the heavy ceramic pot, she placed it on the stovetop and turned to her room.

She sat down on the edge of her narrow bed and retrieved a folio she had hidden between the mattress and the iron base. Opening the folder, she leafed through the pages, examining each one, front and back. She'd been drawing for as long as she could remember, innocent sketches, executed quickly between lessons or homework assignments, or when allowing herself a short break between chores.

What if Mrs. Silverstein was right and this was nothing but heresy? Was she willing to give it all up? With an oblique gaze, she examined the evolving permutation of birds of all colors and shapes. As the borscht started bubbling, she returned to the kitchen and fed the papers to the fire. She watched as the corners blackened and curled, before quickly disintegrating into a heap of ashes.

Pouring two bowls of borscht, she placed one on a silver tray—one of the only items remaining from the Old Country—and took it to her mother's bedroom, setting it down on her bedside table.

"Thank you, Zelda. How was school today?" asked her mother, her voice weak, hair disheveled.

"Dreadful."

Zelda closed the bedroom door behind her and returned to the kitchen. She had no appetite. Particularly not for borscht.

With her mother sick in bed all day long, there was no way she could leave her to study art in Italy, as she'd always imagined she would. She'd be better off giving up on that dream now.

She sat down at the kitchen table and pushed away the bowl of borscht. She opened her notebook and picked up a pen, but instead of copying down the homework assignment, her hand instinctively drew a beak, feathers, a ruffled tail. It was useless trying to give it up. Far from heresy, for her drawing had always been a way of communing with the Divine.

Maybe it would be better to find a private art teacher, a woman who would be sympathetic to her plight and could tutor her after school hours in the privacy of her own home.

She didn't have to give up her faith for her art; she'd find a way to reconcile the two, to sanctify the Divine and express the ineffable. Just as her ancestors had used words to inspire their followers to deepen their spiritual state, she would use brush and paint to accomplish the same.

Zelda's eyes soon closed and her head dropped onto the table as she dozed off, her homework only half done.

—

On her way to school the next morning, as she walked toward the Old City mulling over the excuse she would give Mrs. Silverstein when she inquired why Zelda hadn't completed her homework, Zelda's gaze fell upon an elegant woman wearing a white blouse with puffed sleeves, lace trimming at the collar, and a dark satin skirt with a high waist and a wide belt. Sitting on a stool in front of an easel, holding palette and paintbrush in hand, she was drawing the Old City of Jerusalem with its circular domes, pointed towers, and crenellated walls. Her dark hair was tied back in a tight bun, under a straw hat, secured to her head with a gold hatpin, shading her eyes from the blazing sun.

Zelda was surprised that she had chosen to wear a white blouse for painting and that it was still spotless.

She stopped behind the woman and watched as she applied paint to the canvas, every movement of her hand precise and graceful.

Zelda wanted to skip school and just keep watching the woman at work, but knew she'd get in trouble if she was late or didn't show up at all. Besides, she didn't want to miss morning prayers—she had a lot to atone for this morning.

Mesmerized by the woman's hand movements and by the colorful marks appearing on the canvas, Zelda's feet were glued to the ground, and she couldn't move from her spot.

Just then, another girl wearing the same uniform walked past.

"Hey, Zelda, want to walk together?"

"Why don't you go ahead?" she responded. "I'll catch up soon."

Zelda fell into contemplation. Clearly the woman had no scruples about painting, had never been told that she was committing an unpardonable sin. She wielded her paintbrush as though it were a magic wand, as though she were fulfilling her destiny and making a significant contribution, partaking in the Divine's creation. By engaging in this act, she was doing exactly what she'd been placed on this earth to do—that conviction must have been the source of the confidence she exuded as she painted.

Meanwhile, Zelda's artistic dreams were shattered. It was awful how one well-meaning teacher could ruin one's life ambitions forever.

As though she had eyes in the back of her head, the woman presently turned around and greeted Zelda with a warm smile.

"Good morning! Isn't the sunlight perfect at this time of day?"

Zelda nodded.

"It took me years to get used to the light here in Jerusalem, years in which I wasn't able to paint at all, but now I can't stop myself, it gives me such energy, such joy."

"I love your work. I've always hoped to paint myself."

"I can see you've got a perceptive gaze, so necessary for a painter."

"Really? Do you really think so?" Zelda blushed, her cheeks grew pink like rosebuds about to burst into bloom.

"I recognize in you the same gaze I had at your age in Vienna."

"Will you teach me?" Zelda asked timidly, suddenly growing self-conscious of her Russian accent; the woman was clearly a Yekke—part of the city's German elite. "I've always wanted to learn."

The woman hesitated. "I'm afraid I'm quite busy, but why don't you come over tomorrow evening and I'll introduce you to some of my friends? Maybe one of them will be able to teach you."

"I'd love to; I'd be honored to." The woman jotted down her address on a slip of paper.

Zelda could barely concentrate on her lessons that day at school, nor the next. She was excited to have been invited to the woman's home, and about the prospect of meeting working artists.

As soon as the school bell rang at the end of the following day, Zelda packed up her books in her bookbag and ran home as fast as she could. She hoped to get all her chores done as quickly as possible, so she could get out of the house in time for the artists' meeting that evening. She vigorously scrubbed and cleaned, cooked and fed her mother and made sure she was asleep before slipping out the door. As for herself, she was far too excited to eat anything, her stomach fluttering as though inhabited by a colony of butterflies.

Zelda gently shut the front door of the apartment and ventured out into the deserted street. Jerusalem nights were dark, with very few gas lamps along the way and British soldiers patrolling the dusty streets. One soldier in a smart khaki uniform passed her at that very moment, looked her up and down, his gaze penetrating her figure, even through her modest outfit. He turned his head and followed her with his eyes, sniffing the air as though trying to identify the source of the scent.

Zelda had taken special care about her appearance that evening. She had chosen her fanciest dress, the one made of white taffeta, reserved exclusively for Holy Days, and undid her braids, loosening her hair. Glancing at her reflection in the small bathroom mirror, she thought she still looked like a mere schoolgirl, and quickly retied them.

She had sneaked into her sleeping mother's bedroom and picked up the flask of eau-de-parfum from her dresser, squirting just one spray to her bosom, and then another, for good measure. She'd also found a tube of rouge, and rubbed it on her lips and cheeks. Her mother would never notice; she never had occasion to use it.

It was Zelda's first time attending an adult soirée; her first and (probably) only opportunity to meet working artists, to learn their technique, to be inspired by their work. She worried that she might be late, regretting that she hadn't thought of finding her way in advance in daylight, on her way home from school earlier that day, so that she could locate it more easily in the dark. The Yekke woman looked to her like someone who'd be pedantic about punctuality.

Zelda finally found herself at the gate of the address scribbled on the scrap of paper. She felt sad that she'd burned all of her drawings, having nothing to show tonight.

When the maid opened the front door and ushered her into the salon, Zelda saw that the other guests had already arrived. The maid did nothing to conceal her surprise, her eyebrows raised when she noticed Zelda's youthful face, and she questioned her over and over again to ascertain that she had indeed been invited by the mistress of the house.

Zelda's heart thumped as she approached the salon. She admired the paintings lining every wall and corridor of the house.

She entered the crowded room to hear a heated debate, and found a vacant seat in the corner. She made her way there, trying to make herself as imperceptible as possible. She felt out of place in her modest outfit, in the presence of all these respectable German scholars and accomplished artists. She felt small; intimidated by their presence, by their elegance, and she hadn't even opened her mouth yet. No wonder the maid hadn't believed her at first when she insisted that she'd been invited by none other than Mrs. Ticho herself.

Zelda tried to follow the conversation but felt lost because of the German peppering the Hebrew and the abstract philosophical concepts being discussed. She could appreciate the beauty and originality of the art, each picture featuring its own distinct style.

Staring at the artwork, she felt a radiant sensation she had only ever felt when standing before the Holy One in prayer. She was in awe, nothing more, nothing less, amazed by the beauty that could be created by human hands. Was this heresy?

None of those present at the gathering seemed to be concerned that their art may be heretical. On the contrary, they spoke in such lofty terms, asserting that they were sanctifying God's name by contributing to the consolidation of a unique Jewish culture in the Holy Land, where Jews had finally started to return after two millennia of yearning, working in partnership with God to make the Divine manifest in the world, giving it tangible expression on canvas and paper, a revolutionary movement that could not have come into existence at any other time in history, nor in any other place.

So why was she still trembling with fear that she may be smitten for violating the Second Commandment, when all she was doing was glorifying God's creation, revealing the beauty of the world—more beautiful than anything a flesh and blood artist could possibly have imagined?

Zelda continued observing intently. Just then, a pale, emaciated woman stood up.

Anna introduced her as Rachel the Poetess. Zelda had never heard of her, nor of any other woman writing in Hebrew, for that matter.

"This is Rachel Bluwstein, but she barely needs an introduction. She is simply and endearingly known as Rachel."

I like that, thought Zelda. *Perhaps one day I, too, will simply be known as Zelda. By shedding my surname Schneurson, I won't be bringing any shame upon my dynasty. I'll be free to express myself as my soul desires. My soul will be as free as a bird.*

Zelda noticed that Rachel was more plainly dressed than the others. When she started reading a poem from her notebook, Zelda identified a trace of a Russian accent, just like her own.

But soon Zelda stopped noticing the foreign accent, the clothes, or even her surroundings. She was transported by the woman's voice to higher realms—a mystical experience akin to or even more powerful than reading the words of the Prophets, and sharing in their vision of the Divine. Listening to her descriptions of the Land of Israel and its majestic landscapes, she felt as though the woman were describing not the geography of the land, but the landscape of heaven, of the Garden of Eden.

I'm starting to think that poetry is the most wondrous reality, thought Zelda to herself.

Her words seemed to be composed not of letters and sounds, but of colors and shapes. Zelda closed her eyes and, with every word emitted from the woman's mouth, a different color imprinted itself in her mind's eye.

She was amazed that, despite being a new immigrant herself, she was able to understand Rachel's every word, as she used the simplest vocabulary. Zelda usually struggled so much in Hebrew literature class to understand the poems of the contemporary male poets, who used such dense language and elusive imagery, that left her confused and dumbfounded. She'd even stopped reading the assigned poems at home before class, as she found it a tremendous waste of time, since she neither understood nor retained anything. Only with the teacher's elucidation did the words begin to make sense to her, even though the teacher didn't seem to be endowed with much imagination. Often the poems were as difficult to grasp as the Scriptures, as though the poets considered themselves modern prophets of doom.

What if, like the woman now standing before her, she, too, could paint pictures in words, and use everyday vocabulary to describe the banal joys and sorrows of life? Even the limited vocabulary she currently possessed was sufficient to convey such feelings.

Then no one could possibly say that what she was doing was heresy, as the Bible itself is written in words, composed of the sacred letters of the Hebrew alphabet. Even if she never published a single word, poetry would, no doubt, give her tremendous satisfaction. Hadn't her grandfather, and her great-grandfather before him, inspired their devout followers with the power of words, just by placing one letter next to the other, to reveal the sublime secrets of the universe?

Zelda suddenly became aware of the fragrance of roses suffusing the salon, penetrating the open window from Anna's flourishing garden. She'd noticed on her way in how beautiful it was, how lush, despite the darkness that prevented her from identifying the diverse species.

As the fragrance grew stronger, Zelda noticed a vase on the corner table containing a few pale pink roses. *In poetry, it isn't about the rose*, she pondered, *but rather its fragrance, its radiance, the sensation it arouses in the reader.* Closing her eyes, she allowed her spirit to soar, until the end of the recitation brought her firmly back to the salon.

I've never read poetry by a Jewish woman, except perhaps Deborah the Prophetess in the Book of Judges. Rachel's poetry is the first modern Hebrew verse by a woman that I know. I wish I could be like her, writing in Hebrew about women's everyday reality.

Though secular Jews may not be interested in descriptions of my religious lifestyle—the sheen of the Shabbat candles, the texture of braided challah, the taste of ritual wine—they may, nonetheless, find themselves moved if only they could perceive my poetry for what it really is, a portal to God, each word, each letter, a manifestation of Divine presence. Just as Rachel glorifies the landscape of the Land of Israel, so, too, will I glorify the small daily blessings and wonders of God's creation. Thus, not only will I not be an embarrassment to my Hasidic dynasty, I will also be exalting its legacy, making manifest the unique melody of each and every blade of grass.

As Rachel sat down to catch her breath, Zelda, too, needed to catch hers, so exhilarated was she by the recitation. Soon after the gathering dispersed, and she worked up the courage to approach Rachel: "Will I see you again?" she asked. "Would you read and comment on some of my poems?"

"Unlikely," responded the poetess, her breath shallow. "I'm afraid I am at the end of my days; but I encourage you to explore and discover your own voice. I would urge you to read a chapter of the Bible each day—there is no greater teacher of writing."

If I ever gain fame as a poet, I'll repay Mrs. Ticho's kindness in inviting me here tonight by taking young girls under my wing and mentoring them. If I ever have a daughter of my own, I'll make sure to let her know that she can realize her wildest dreams; I'll be sure to instill in her a love of art and literature, rather than the fear of God.

As the salon emptied of guests, Zelda plucked a rose from the vase on the corner table and, turning her head to ascertain that no one was watching, inserted it into the buttonhole of her plain gray sweater. The fragrance of the rose followed her as she thanked Anna for her hospitality and left the glowing warmth of the house. It continued to suffuse her as she walked down the dark streets back to the dingy apartment she shared with her mother.

Looking down at the pink bud she had sneaked out as a souvenir, it took on the appearance of a black rose in the darkness of the night. Inhaling deeply, she thought to herself: *Isn't the scent of roses the essence of poetry?* as her very first verses formed in her mind to the rhythm of her steps against the stone pavement:

Did my longing create
The black rose you gave me
In my dream?

Degeneration

Every child in Germany knows how I bestowed honor on our people there.

—Else Lasker-Schüler

Else entered the tiny studio on Regalstrasse, slamming the door behind her. She collapsed on one of the only pieces of furniture in the room, the stiff brown couch which also served as her bed and writing desk, bumping her already bruised head against the armrest.

"Ouch," she exclaimed, shifting to find a less painful position, but could find none. Whichever way she turned she landed on another wound.

Lounging on the sofa from which he barely moved, her only child, Paul, exhaled shallow breaths. Despite his weakness, anxiety over his mother's whereabouts had kept him awake. Taking her hand in his, he kissed his mother's bruised arm.

Even Paul's soft lips exacerbated the pain, like the lips of the angel guarding Jerusalem, its kisses simultaneously soothing and burning. "Thank you, my darling, but you must not strain yourself. I'll be fine; it's better already."

Else wore a torn and stained silver gown that shimmered in the moonlight, which entered the chamber through the tiny window near the ramshackle ceiling. This was the sole source of illumination for the artist and her son at this late hour, besides the two thin flames of the Sabbath candles, which she had kindled in the hanging brass *Judenstern* before leaving the house. They kept vigil until her return, reminding her of the sanctity she had left behind earlier that evening. Two columns of wax once a week, though the star-shaped lamp called for six, were the only luxuries she allowed herself in this time of recession, when electricity was sporadic. The moonlight was sufficient to illuminate Else's *Kleist Prize*, the only ornament on the faded, peeling wallpaper. The flames flickered against the certificate, illuminating one letter at a time, first the name of the prize, Germany's highest literary honor, then her own name, and finally the date, barely three months before.

"The next stop can only be exile," she lamented, flinging her head even farther back until the strain hurt her neck. "That's the only reason I agreed to attend tonight's ball and paint his portrait for the Reichstag."

"What happened, Mother? Why did you respond to his summons?" asked Paul.

"This commission might have brought me enough money to purchase breakfast for us and antibiotics for you tomorrow morning, but I suppose that now we must go hungry again ... for the third day in a row."

"Don't worry about me, Mother."

"I know how much you are suffering, Paul, but I simply cannot afford painkillers this week," she caressed his translucent, frozen cheek, her fingers sinking into the hollow.

Else shuddered as she recalled how the officer had seized her by the braid and pulled her to her feet, while they were alone in the parlor where she painted his portrait. Still holding onto her hair, he looked her up and down, examining every inch of her emaciated body, prodding her protruding ribs and chin. He then flung her to the floor with disgust and asked, "What are you good for, anyway? Not only can you not paint properly, but even your body isn't worth my attention."

She noticed Paul's sidelong glance, his eyes wide open for the first time in months, examining her scratched face. But he kept quiet, as was his custom. Even producing the softest of sounds strained his lungs and winded him. He seemed paler and more fragile than ever, like a porcelain figurine. "Don't worry, my dear, I'd much rather retain my dignity than be fed by a Nazi," she assured him, kissing his forehead.

She closed her eyes to alleviate her pounding headache, but a sequence of the night's events immediately replayed against her eyelids. As much as Else hated the officer—for Else had this insight, as artists often do, and could see right through his eyes and straight into his heart—the portrait she had begun to paint of him on the finest canvas she could obtain was, technically speaking, one of her best artworks to date. A harmony of colors reigned on the canvas, accentuating the perfect proportions of the figure against the background.

She delineated the contours of his torso with charcoal and added shiny purple eyes, elongated blood-orange hands, and a square green moustache. She then flattened the figure by filling in the outline with dark brown paint. The right half of the face she painted pink, and the left half she colored blue. Else could not restrain herself and filled the background with thick brushstrokes of bright orange, yellow and red, intertwined with the officer's angular physique. It was the first painting in twenty years from which she excluded the white stones and golden domes of Jerusalem; Pharaoh was undeserving of such a sacred site, "*God's veiled bride, the observatory of the hereafter, the heaven before Heaven*," drowning in the Sea of Reeds on his way.

She thought of Franz, the art shop owner on the corner of her street, who agreed to open the back door of his little shop after-hours so that she could replenish her supply, even though it endangered both his life and hers. He charged her only a nominal fee beyond his own expenses and allowed her to take supplies on credit. He knew she did not have the cash now but assumed that the masterpieces she would paint on his canvases would eventually enable her to compensate him tenfold, after the collapse of the regime. Then everyone would know the source of her tightly woven, pristine canvases; their fine texture shone through the paint, making all the difference between mediocre and outstanding works.

She recalled how Franz used to sit in the corner of the Romanisches Café in her days of glory, listening to her poetry recitations. He would lean forward, afraid to miss a single syllable of her soft, hushed tone, glaring at the pastry eater at the next table who noisily chewed his *Mandelbrot*. The bitterness of his coffee was sweetened by her melodious voice, conjuring exotic worlds with no props other than her boa. Climbing onto a table, she alone of the café's patrons permitted to do so, she would mime her words, the entire length of her body undulating to the rhythm of her poem *Shulamite*. Embodying the biblical princess, King Solomon's beloved, she knotted her scarf as a tiara around her black tresses, reciting:

"*O, from your sweet mouth
I learned too much of bliss!*"

Hiding behind his ceramic mug and *Berliner Morgenpost*, he illustrated the scene in his sketchbook. In the center, he sketched her portrait, enthroned as Prince Jussuf among her people, only a select few of whom she admitted into her inner circle and endowed with rope diadems matching hers. He prided himself on how he had captured her facial expression and considered it his masterpiece; it hung on the wall behind the shop counter, demonstrating to his customers all that could be accomplished with his products.

He surprised her with the framed portrait the next time she entered his shop. It brought an instant sparkle to her eyes and a spontaneous *"Wunderbar!"* Even in her impulsiveness, she lost none of her regal bearing. So thrilled was he by her response that he gave her a huge discount that day, and a complimentary bottle of turpentine. He had been offering her discounts ever since.

Tonight she had been "offered the privilege" of painting the officer's portrait—while other artists of her tribe were forbidden to paint at all as they were considered of lowly race—at such short notice that she did not have the chance to notify Franz. When she swung by his shop on her way to the Reichstag, he had already locked up and left for home. Circling the shop, Else discovered a back window partly open. Looking left and right to ensure that no one spied on her, she hoisted herself onto the windowsill. She heard a long tear as her stiletto heel caught the hem of her dress. She couldn't present herself at her commission in a torn gown, but there was no time to go back and change, nor any dress in better condition at home—this had been her very best. She pushed the window open and climbed into the little shop. Landing safely among the objects of her passion, she grabbed hold of scissors from the counter and cut ten inches from the entire circumference of her gown, exposing her ankles and part of her calves, to camouflage the tear.

Guided only by the moonlight, and by her familiarity with the contents of the store, she was drawn to the canvases. Remembering that they were arranged on the shelves by increasing size and quality, she raised her arm as high as she could reach and pulled down a medium-sized square canvas of the purest white cotton. Running her fingers along its surface to confirm its trademark smoothness, she rolled it up and stuck it into her purse. She then pulled open the gouache drawer and grabbed a small tube of each primary color: red, yellow, and blue. She threw them into her purse, adding them to the pastels she had brought from home. Shaking her empty wallet, she left the strip of silvery satin on the counter by the cash register, as a deposit. Franz knew her limited wardrobe intimately; he would recognize the owner of the dress without any more explicit identification, which could endanger them both in the event of a Nazi inspection. Else used a stool to climb onto the windowsill and jumped into the courtyard, leaving the window wide open behind her.

Even the refinement of the canvas could not rescue her from the officer's wrath. Or perhaps it was specifically its fine quality, forbidden to "degenerate" Jewish artists such as herself, which angered him. His curiosity aroused by the violent motions of her paintbrush, the officer rose from his seat and peeked at the portrait. So engrossed was she in her work that she did not notice the officer's approach until he stomped his foot, furious at seeing his character thus revealed. Startled, she raised her eyes from the canvas, just as the officer pulled the Party's artistic regulations from his pocket and reminded her of his desire to be glorified in a regal manner. He pointed to the wall behind her, where his self-portrait hung. It was modeled on Jean-Auguste-Dominique Ingres's *Napoleon Enthroned*, except that the officer had substituted a swastika for the eagle emblem and given the emperor his own facial features. Else's sharp eye discerned the shakiness of the lines and the tonal disharmony, which further distinguished the officer's self-portrait from Ingres's masterpiece, but decided that it would be unwise to point these deficiencies out to him.

"That's what I want to see. Do you understand? All those who wish to be recognized as German artists must from now on produce the kind of art I sanction," he declared. "How dare you render an Aryan body less than perfect, even deformed?"

Else refused to compromise and alter her style at his demand. She put down her paintbrush, crossed her arms, and turned her back to the Nazi.

The officer sneered, silently celebrating his triumph over her. "That's it; this will be the end of your career, as well as that of all your Jewish friends from the Expressionist movement. I will no longer tolerate your incitement of the German people against the Party through your so-called art," he threatened. Else shivered; her spine tense and stiff. "Only a true German with the blood of a thousand Aryan generations running through their veins could maintain the greatness of German art. You're corrupting its purity and destroying the aesthetic that this most illustrious of nations has labored for centuries to achieve, all because you're incapable of such greatness," he hissed.

Else opened her mouth to explain the value of abstraction according to such celebrated German authorities as

Immanuel Kant and G.W.F. Hegel but was interrupted by the officer. "It's no use shunning the classical style and initiating a new artistic movement. We all know that you aspire to paint like the Masters but are simply incapable of it, and refuse to admit that; incapable because you are producing on stolen land where you have no roots."

"Max Liebermann, who heads the Prussian Academy of Arts, is Jewish, too," she protested.

"The days of his presidency are numbered," responded the officer.

Rearranging herself on the threadbare sofa, Else realized that the Nazi officer had not chosen her as his portraitist in order to honor her, nor due to his admiration of her art. "He'd seen my work before," she recollected aloud, forgetting that her grown son was within earshot, "at the exhibition featuring this year's winners of the Weimar Art Academy Competition. I should have remembered the insults his men spray-painted on the walls above our paintings; deliberately allowing the spray to drip onto our prize canvases. I should have known that no one is permitted to espouse individual feelings anymore. That is my greatest crime, he proclaimed in his degrading speech tonight, besides my being Jewish, of course."

To ensure that Else did not depart from the hall right away, the Nazi officer grabbed her by the wrists, spilling the pigments from her palette all over her dress. He then forced her to her feet and dragged her to the middle of the dance floor. Clasping her tightly to his chest, they moved their feet mechanically and out of synch to Richard Wagner's *Faust Overture*, performed by a string quartet in military uniform. Every note sent a shiver through Else's body. Her knees shook and she was forced to lean closer into the officer to hold herself upright, feeling more and more repulsed with every step.

The officer finally let go of his solid grasp of her to make his way to the podium. Else commanded her legs to regain their firmness and carry her through the hall to the heavy doors, but the narrow stiffness of the dress hindered her motion, delaying her escape. She was detained at the exit by armed guards.

An easel concealed behind a thick red curtain stood in the middle of the platform. The officer slammed his fist into the podium. "You are about to witness the so-called 'artwork' of a degenerate," he announced.

Pulling the curtain aside, the officer unveiled Else's portrait. A stunned silence filled the auditorium. People remained frozen, couples detached themselves from one another, spun into frontal view and stared, jaws dropping open. They were mesmerized by the painting's powerful color scheme and skillful structure, but most of all by its portrayal of the full complexity of the officer's personality, who they all pretended to adore, but before whom they quivered.

The officer roared, "I see you're all of the same mind as myself. There is no applause, nor a single exclamation of approbation, as this painting is unworthy of it. In fact, all it merits is laughter."

As though on cue, the crowd erupted into laughter; softly at first, each man checking his neighbor's reaction, and then with greater vigor. The officer was so pleased that his own laughter rose above all of theirs. It continued to resound across the auditorium long after their forced laughter had subsided.

Once he regained his composure, the officer approached the easel. Pointing a rigid finger to the canvas, he began, "The reason this so-called painting aroused such laughter, my dear compatriots, is its unfinished state, which some second-class artists call 'abstraction'." Raising his arm to the canvas, "Observe here how the painter's use of non-continuous lines and short brushstrokes destroys the integrity of the painting. Further, her juxtaposition of complementary colors is a strain on the eye, while the body that disintegrates into the background is unnatural. Instead of reveling in the beauty of a healthy Aryan body, it dissolves into impasto. I am telling you, it is all part of the barbaric conspiracy to defile German culture." The men in uniform in the front row nodded their heads in unison.

"Therefore, ladies and gentlemen, we have requested an accomplished artist to complete this unfinished painting. I welcome the newly appointed *Künstlerischer Leiter*, Kaspar Häusner, Germany's Artistic Leader." As he stepped onto the platform in his tuxedo, Else recognized the freckled man who had sat behind her in art school, always copying her compositions and distracting her with dirty jokes, until he was expelled at the end of the second year. It turned out that the portfolio he had submitted to the admissions committee had been prepared by his uncle. While she and other graduates of their class had gone on to establish avant-garde movements and sell their paintings to national museums around the globe, he worked at a soda factory.

As their eyes met, his lips contorted and his eyes shone triumphantly. His expression chilled her. Removing his jacket and rolling up his sleeves, he pulled a palette knife out of his belt. The audience gasped. Else winced and turned her head, placing one hand on her chest and the other on her abdomen. She bent forward to delay the rise of the nausea as he scratched out the officer's face with swift scraping motions. The officer exclaimed "cut it all out, scrape it all off, leave no trace of that filth!" Else felt as though a knife was piercing her heart. The replacement blew on the canvas to disperse the residue of her pigments.

Placing a photograph of the officer on the easel next to the canvas, he began to fill Else's outline with beige, concealing the acne scars and the mole on his cheek. He gave the officer uncrossed blue eyes, which everyone, even from afar, could see he did not possess, and a lighter tone of brown hair with golden highlights. After straightening and narrowing his nose, he added a gold crown surmounted by an eagle with outspread wings and pinned a swastika to his gray uniform. Kaspar then cleared Else's colorful background and replaced it with the officer's own design of the Temple of Art, a classical, colonnaded building with a marble portico.

After signing his name, Häusner stepped aside, an outstretched hand indicating the refurbished portrait, and said, "I present to you the official portrait of our beloved General Lieutenant."

The officer rose from his throne to inspect the canvas. "Now *this* is a true German painting!" He clapped Kaspar's back with his left hand while shaking his right hand vigorously. "I am proud to hold the hand of a true German artist," he declared. Applause thundered through the hall as two muscular men lifted the canvas from the easel and hung it on a nail above the officer's seat.

The doors opened and the crowd departed. Else attempted to camouflage herself among them, intending to make her way to the freedom of the street, but the guard recognized her and seized her by the strap of her dress, dragging her into the courtyard, where the people had reassembled. The iron gates remained locked.

A tall bonfire danced in the center of the courtyard, glowing orange with the pages torn out of books and fed to it. A sheet of paper flew loose in the wind, and landed in Else's hand. She instantly recognized her poem "Homesickness":

Who will anoint my dead palaces—
They wore the crowns of my fathers,
Whose prayers drowned in the holy river.

The poem was accompanied by her own illustration of *Thebes with Jussuf*, the prince's profile looking out of a blue window in a crowded neighborhood of domes and stars. Else let out a loud shriek. The guard punched her ear. She almost fell over. Her entire body trembled. She wished she could flee, but she was paralyzed. One guard grabbed her by the dress, while another pulled her by her hair toward the fire. As she was unable to move, her dress tore and a handful of her already sparse hair remained in the guard's fist. When they reached the center of the circle, he threw it into the fire.

His hands free, he collected the books (no doubt the price of admission to the night's gala), from the crowd, and piled them beside the fire. Else noticed that those in the inner circle each held at least five of her books. For a moment she felt proud as she recalled the days when her books were best-sellers and everyone recited her poetry.

If they had each read half the books they held, they knew her spirit intimately. How could they do this to her? Had her words not had the intended humanizing effect? What was the point of poetry otherwise? Didn't it teach them to empathize with her as a Jew, as an artist, as a woman, as a German, as a human being? She had failed as a poet; of course she deserved to have her books burned, she thought, *if they did not move people to greater compassion.*

The fire, which warmed her at first (she had abandoned her shawl in the gallery), now charred her skin. She felt her cheeks getting scorched. Raising a hand to her face, she could not feel her fingers against the burnt patches, having lost all sensation. She stood there, gasping for air.

As the guard received the books from the people, he tore the pages out of the binding, and handed them to another guard to Else's left. The second guard would read verses, selected at random, before crumpling up the page and throwing it into the fire, to the crowd's raucous cheers.

"The rock decays
From which I spring
To sing my songs of God."

As the sound of the syllables reached her ears, Else's eyelids shut and her lips parted. Her tongue twisted in her mouth, silently forming the words. She saw herself back at the Romanisches Café amid a large crowd of admirers. Soon her high voice overtook his deep monotone and he grew silent, allowing her to complete the recitation, replete with her usual sweeping gestures and swaying motions.

"And still, still the echo
In me,
When to the East, awesomely,
The decaying rock of bone,
My people,
Cries out to God."

Else fell to her knees and ended the performance with both hands over her heart, a plea for mercy. She was overwhelmed by the silence that now permeated the courtyard; a silence she had not thought possible in the presence of so many.

The guard was the first to recover his voice. He booed. One by one, the others joined in his cry, drowning her out in a tonal wave. She was captured in the sea of voices, her poetic words reverberating inside her.

A tome hit her head, knocking her to the ground, and brought her out of her trance. She picked it up from the asphalt, where it had landed, and opened it to the title page. She recognized her own handwritten dedication to her beloved friend, Gottfried Benn, a fellow Expressionist poet. A tear trickled down her cheek for the first time that evening at the realization that he was among them. Wasn't it he who had called her the "greatest lyrical poet Germany ever had," and who had dedicated his second book of poetry, *Söhne*, to her? Didn't he, just a few months before, send her a note, which she had memorized: *"the Kleist Prize, so often sullied, was once again ennobled by being awarded to you. Congratulations to German poetry!"* Had he always been insincere, or had they simply brainwashed him?

Still on the ground, Else leafed through the pages, illuminated by the towering flames behind her. *Hebrew Ballads* was her favorite book. She found comfort in the poems and illustrations she had produced with the same fountain pen. She traced the contours of the images with her forefinger and caressed the vellum of the cover, warming her numb hand. She attempted to focus her eyes on the words, to lull herself with their rhythm, to shut out the infernal scene at the heart of which she sat, but was distracted and dizzied by the chaos. She shut the book and slipped it down the front of her dress.

Crawling on all fours with her head lowered to avoid the flying books, she slithered through the stomping legs until she reached the gate. There a guard obstructed her passage and pulled her to her feet. Noticing the bulge in her chest, he reached into her dress, squeezed her breast and snatched the book. Smacking her back with it, he threw her onto the street like a sacrificial lamb sent out of Jerusalem into the Valley of Hinnom, as the magnificent Temple burned to ashes behind her.

She ran down the road along the stone wall which enclosed the Reichstag and heard feet shuffling within. Peering over the wall as she paused for breath, she heard the men chanting "Death to the Jews," "Deutschland for Aryans" and "Aryan beauty is perfection." She imagined that, her disappearance noted, they had convinced themselves they had pushed her into the fire and burned her, along with her corrupt books and degenerate paintings, punishing her as the witch they believed her to be.

When she entered her studio, out of breath, Else kicked the easel with her stiletto heel before collapsing onto the couch beside her son. She breathed a sigh of relief as she resolved to leave Germany forever and relocate to Palestine, and more specifically to Jerusalem, the city that "*blesses those who long for its blessing, the devout city comforts those who wish to be comforted.*" She knew that there, artists like herself would possess the freedom to paint as they wished, incorporating Jewish themes with vivid colors, rather than having their artworks censored, as in Germany.

Before starting her life anew in that distant country, so close to her heart, she rummaged through her purse and pulled out the three containers of gouache and two pastel sticks she had managed to smuggle out of the Reichstag. She lifted the floorboards and retrieved a small scrap of canvas, no larger than a postcard, left over from her most acclaimed painting, *Bunch of Wild Jews*, produced less than a year before. She unfolded her three-legged bedside table and placed the scrap of canvas on the narrow ledge. She struck a match, lit another candle and shut the curtains, fearful that a Nazi patrol would see the light and suspect that she was again painting against regulations.

She drew a flattened woman with cropped black hair dressed in a torn and stained silver gown. Wearing red stud earrings and a pearl necklace, the woman balanced uncomfortably on a wooden stool. Eyes shut, back curved, head tilted forward, she held a paintbrush in her right hand, while her left forearm, covered in bruises, was supported by a younger figure whose ivory hand offered her a red rose. Behind them, the background was divided in two: the left-hand side somber with a hefty neoclassical portico, while a golden stone building decorated with blue mosaics hovered on the right-hand side, its domes and pointed arches piercing the clouds. The two sections were cleft by long yellow and orange brushstrokes, consuming the buildings.

Turning to her motionless son, eager to share her painting with him, she touched his forehead and found it to be cold. As she reached for his wrist under the blanket, a small piece of cardboard fell out of his hand, left over from her sketch of *Jussuf Sculpts His Mother*. She made out a soft pencil outline of her profile, with spots on the neck and chest, no doubt executed under the quilt as she sat there next to him, contemplating the night's events.

Else dropped the cardboard and placed her own painting in Paul's other hand. She wanted to run out for help, but feared that she would be arrested and beaten for breaking curfew so late at night. Helpless, she collapsed on the edge of the couch and cradled her son in her arms. Supporting his neck, she smoothed back his oily hair and traced his facial features with her index finger, deliberately committing them to memory. She felt his heartbeat slow and weaken, as silent tears rolled down her cheeks.

When she could no longer feel his pulse, she pulled the blanket up to his chin and placed his cardboard drawing in her clutch purse, along with her most recent self-portrait and the *Kleist Prize* certificate, which she unhooked from the wall. She folded the easel and lifted the wooden floorboards with her remaining strength, tucking away the pastels and tubes of gouache. Wrapping a wool scarf over her stained, torn, almost translucent gown, she walked out of the studio with only her purse in her hand.

—

The same Jerusalem that I have glorified so in my poems offers me no home.

Else stood at the cracked mirror, the only one in her studio apartment on HaMa'alot Street. Though the bright sun rays refracting from the glass blinded her, she could see the crenellated reflection of the Old City of Jerusalem. It was so hot that Else had fully opened the windows and shutters to let in the breeze. The song of the sparrows soothed her until she heard a shriek. Rushing to the window, she saw a man in a *keffiyeh* wielding a knife at a child with side curls.

Shutting the window to block out the noise, she returned to the mirror, where she started dressing for the evening's event, though many hours remained. She had isolated herself for months while composing her most recent collection of poetry, *My Blue Piano*, and was excited about returning to the society of German artists. She wished to make a good impression and to uphold the reputation she had established for herself back in Europe.

She imagined herself at the Romanisches Café, among fervent admirers, reciting her newest poems and displaying the accompanying lithographs. Many of those who would be present tonight had been part of that crowd, and they were somehow to reunite here in the holiest of cities, to celebrate the greatness of German poetry. It had been such a long time since she had held court as Prince Jussuf and carried her audience to exotic lands. She was eager to escape to the heavenly Jerusalem she had not yet attained, despite her prolonged residence in its worldly incarnation.

Opening her dusty old suitcase, untouched in months, she pulled the garments out one by one. Examining the material, front and back, for moth holes, she threw them onto her narrow bed in two distinct piles: the wearable and the memorable. She did not take the heat wave into account while assembling her outfit, selecting one item for each poem she intended to read. Her art always took precedence over her personal comfort.

Despite the oppressive heat, she slipped on a brown wool dress, then a burgundy tweed vest and a black velvet jacket. Once she was fully dressed, after trying and rejecting numerous garments in the process, she turned to her accessory box and picked out a pearl necklace and an ivory brooch carved with

Paul's profile, as well as her favorite pink boa. As she could not decide between a red leather cap and an indigo felt hat, she wore both, one on top of the other. She completed the outfit with her fake ankle-high alligator boots, the only sturdy pair remaining in her possession.

She lugged a large cardboard box filled to the brim with freshly minted copies of her newest book. Its weight bowed her neck and shoulders, slowed her down, and disrupted the regularity of her breath. She was forced to stop every few feet, put the box down, and rest, inhaling deeply. She was glad she had left her apartment early; she would reach the Tichos' house just in time. Sweat dripped from her forehead and seeped through the many layers of clothes, emitting a sour odor.

Each time she paused, bunches of children would congregate around her and point nasty fingers at her. They would giggle and stoop to pick up whatever stones or garbage lay at their feet: cigarette butts, candy wrappers or fragments of glass bottles, and take aim at her. The multiple layers of clothes padded her torso and softened the impact. She did not have the energy to chase those kids, as she had so many times before.

She did not mind carrying the books, even as she climbed the steep hill to the Tichos' grand home. She was certain that they would be bestsellers that night, just like her previous collections of poetry. She was pleased to have published another volume, certainly her last. The publishers seemed to have forgotten her name, only ten years before the talk of all cultured men. Even homeless men used to recite her poetry.

Now Else was the only one who had the poems memorized and she would recite them all by herself. She rose from the sofa that had been vacated for her upon her arrival at the salon, out of respect for her greatness, no doubt. She climbed onto the sofa, her scaly green heels digging into the upholstery as she swayed to stabilize herself, but the others did not stop their chattering even as she recited the opening lines of her poem "Jerusalem":

"God formed out of his spine: Palestine
Out of one single bone: Jerusalem."

Clearing her throat to catch their attention, she tried once more:

"Our holy city turned to stone."

As she paused for breath, a Hebrew University professor yelled, "Would you refrain from scratching our ears with those awful sounds? How could anyone in their right mind still perceive beauty in the harsh, guttural cadences of the German murderers? How about some inspirational Hebrew poetry?"

"A poet cannot write in any language but his or her mother tongue," whispered Else in response, but her words were subsumed in the growing chatter.

Anna, the hostess, ran to Else's aid, helping her down from the sofa. "Hear her out," she commanded. "Some respect for Germany's greatest poetess."

"Why are you defending one who has copied your painting technique?" retorted the scholar. "It is no coincidence that the cover image is of the Jerusalem landscape from Talpiyot, depicted in the same minimalist, linear way, with a similar emphasis on barren hills, domed structures, and the native population."

"Else's style could never be like anyone else's," asserted Anna. "It's too original, too distinct. Please, continue." Anna nodded in her direction.

"Yes, so original, like a little child's," the scholar chuckled, as Else proceeded with her recitation, strengthened by Anna who stood guard at her side.

"Were you to come ...
My arm would encircle you, framing a holy image."

Laughter erupted from the corner of the room and spread throughout, rekindling that buried suffering in Else's heart. She bent over, delaying the rise of the nausea to her throat and concealing her blushing cheeks. She continued in a shaky voice. Her lower lip trembled. If the words had not made them laugh before, their ruffled delivery certainly would now.

"Were you to come—
To this ancestral land—
You would reproach me like a little child:
Jerusalem, arise and live again!"

A tear rolled down Else's cheek as she pronounced the final words. Anna and Albert Ticho's applause resounded in the hollowness of the vaulted salon, emphasizing their singularity. Men rose from their seats and approached her; to congratulate her privately, she expected. Finally, her words had touched the tenderest hearts, though they only represented a minority.

Instead, voices rose from afar, "How can one denigrated by the Nazis still strive for an aesthetic of which she has been deemed unworthy, incapable? Don't you know it's immoral to delude readers with the semantic smoothness of German words?"

Only a fellow poet offered a solution, in a soft, hesitant voice, "Will you grant me permission to translate your poems into Hebrew?"

"There's no need," she replied, waving her hand. "They already are in Hebrew, in the language of the Psalms and Prophets. Would you like to purchase a copy?"

"This is no place to peddle your goods," reprimanded the scholar. "Get out of here." He kicked the cardboard box. The books dispersed all over the floor. Else collapsed onto her hands and knees to recuperate them, as Anna attempted to quieten the uproar and disperse the crowd.

Else limped all the way home, carrying the box full of books, after the heel broke from the sole of her boot as she ran out of the house and down the pebbly garden path. She felt so disgraced that she refused to allow Doctor Ticho to lend her a supporting shoulder and accompany her.

As she crossed King George V Boulevard, she noticed a pack of black crows with hooked beaks gnawing ravenously on the bloody body of a cat crushed to death. Flattened in the middle of the road, the birds fought over the fleshiest portions, pushing rivals away by spreading their wings. Whenever a car drove past, they would rise like a black feather cape, only to dive down again and cover the cat in their blackness, pecking its green eyes out.

Back at the drawing table, nauseated in a room by now cold and clammy, Else opened her cotton purse, punctured with holes left by the unraveling threads, and removed the postcard-sized wooden portfolio. It was one of the very few possessions, and by far the most prized, that had accompanied her overseas from Berlin to Jerusalem. She had been forced to abandon all her other belongings to the Nazis.

They wouldn't find much, in any case. They were unlikely to search under the floorboards, but with such greedy brutes as they, one could never know. They would have all her books and paintings—those they hadn't already burned to ashes, that is—pretending they were valueless in order to justify auctioning them off to foreign collectors, to enrich their coffers, and finance the atrocities they carried out against her people. *Mein Volk.*

The postcard-sized canvas, the last she had painted in her homeland, had remained with her like an open heart, recording the scars inflicted by the Nazi autocracy. Adhering to its back was Paul's cardboard profile of her, the very last product of his hands.

She examined the canvas. The Jerusalem of gold she had yearned for did not exist, nor did the sanctity she had imagined, or the peace she had fantasized about. Using charcoal, Else grounded the foundations of the domed stone structures in the background, adding shadows and incising wrinkles on the figure's face and neck. She thinned and silvered her hair with white chalk. A red pastel stick withered the rose held out to her by her son, amassing a pile of petals on the ground. Using her favorite fountain pen, she scribbled in the margin of the canvas: *"the blessed land needed a poet to come extol it."*

Rings of Smoke

I have conceived nothing but poetry.

—Leah Goldberg

Leah sat on the balcony overlooking the Mediterranean Sea, rings of smoke floating from her cigarette, blurring the crisp sapphire blue of the sea on the horizon.

Her mother, Tsila, came out to the balcony, suspended on Bauhaus columns, carrying a tray with two steaming cups of Turkish coffee.

"Thank you, Mother," Leah said, extending her hand to pick up her cup.

"Anything I can do to help you concentrate on your writing."

Leah dropped her cigarette onto the ashtray in the middle of the round table and raised the cup to her lips, sipping the steaming brown liquid. She felt the caffeine coursing through her veins, while the tobacco served as a calming antidote.

The cup still raised to her lips, she turned her head to gaze out to sea so that her mother could only see her profile.

"I know I'll miss Tel Aviv once we've moved to the capital next week!"

"So will I," responded Tsila. "But look on the bright side. Maybe there you'll meet a suitable young man and finally make me a grandmother. Wasn't there a young poet you admired in Jerusalem?"

"Perhaps, but you know I made a firm decision not to marry when Father's illness erupted. It would be cruel to impose such a fate on any child."

"A fate worse than death, certainly, and terribly hereditary. Nonetheless, Leah, my dear, perhaps you'll allow yourself to open your heart to another, one day. Your poems are so sad. Soon they'll be calling you the poet of the broken heart."

"I thought that one day I would have someone to write for," admitted Leah with a sigh. She put her cup down on the table and picked up her cigarette again, inhaling deeply. "Besides the sea, I'll miss the group of poets I met with regularly here in Tel Aviv. I was the only woman invited to join. That's where I learned to chain smoke and drink alcohol like a man, at the small café on Dizengoff Street, where we used to meet."

"I wouldn't say those are such good habits you picked up," remarked Tsila, waving her hand in the air to chase away the smoke.

"I am, of course, proud of all the poetry books you've published, but could anything replace progeny of flesh and blood?"

The sun began its descent into the sea.

Noticing that her daughter had put her cup down, Tsila rose to her feet and rushed inside to boil more water.

"They've invited me to join the faculty of the Hebrew University as a scholar of Russian literature, not as a poet in my own right. Perhaps no one in Jerusalem even knows my poetry."

"I have no doubt they've all read your work, Leah."

"They have a style of their own there, a different manner of speech altogether. What if I don't have time to compose poetry when I am busy preparing lectures and writing scholarly papers and literary criticism? Poetry is my true passion; will I now have to set it aside?" Leah paused as she pondered, taking a deep breath.

"I will do everything in my power to enable you to write," pledged Tsila.

"Even though I studied in Berlin, those Yekke scholars at the Hebrew University do not regard me as one of their own."

"I'm sure you'll soon earn their respect."

"It seems that literary taste in Jerusalem is more conservative than it is here in Tel Aviv. Here I was part of the avant-garde, leading a poetic revolution. Who knows, there I might just be on the fringe of the literary establishment."

"Have no fear, Leah, and stay true to your vision."

The sun was low on the horizon, and the light dimmed. Leah extinguished her cigarette and closed her voluminous copy of Tolstoy's *War and Peace*, which she had just started translating into Hebrew.

"Good night, Mother." She retired to her bedroom, leaving the older woman alone in the kitchen to wash the day's dishes.

Leah and Tsila spent the following week packing their belongings. When the open-roof truck arrived to collect their baggage and transport it to Jerusalem, the majority of the boxes contained Leah's vast library of Russian, German, and Hebrew books, as well as unsold copies of her three poetry collections.

That morning Leah had walked down to the seashore, to say goodbye to the Mediterranean. She sat on the sandy beach for two hours, notebook in one hand, pen in the other, writing a letter to the sea she loved so dearly, watching the light change as the sun rose higher into the sky, waves glimmering under it.

Leah removed her shoes and socks, allowing her feet to sink into the hot sand. The soft grains tickled her toes. She removed her long, loose, linen dress, pulling it over her head to reveal a modest black bathing suit covering not only her torso, but also her thighs and upper arms. Throwing her clothes in a heap on the beach, the neutral tones camouflaged by the sand, she stepped toward the shoreline and dipped her body in the cool water—at first, tentatively, just her toes, and then, as she took a step forward, she submerged her legs. She continued stepping deeper and deeper into the water as though ritually cleansing herself in preparation for ascending the Judean Mountains and entering the sanctitude of Jerusalem.

When she came out of the water, she dried herself with a towel, whose fibers had grown coarse from years of airdrying. She stood radiant under the sunlight and bathed in its glowing warmth.

After returning home, she took one last shower in her Tel Aviv apartment, savoring the saltiness of the drops landing on her tongue. The water in Jerusalem was no doubt sweeter, being so very far away from the sea.

—

The trek up the Judean Hills in the open-roof truck took all day, after it repeatedly stalled and the motor had to be reignited in defiance of gravity. The steep ascent was difficult. Leah found comfort in the knowledge that she was surrounded by her cherished books and would soon have a new landscape to inspire her poetry. She had loved composing poetry in Hebrew ever since she was a little girl. If she couldn't write for an extended period of time, her heart would break. She had heard that Jerusalemites speak Hebrew differently from the rest of the country, use different vocabulary. Would her poems still resonate with them?

Leah rested her head against her mother's shoulder, just as she had done as a little girl crossing the Russian border. The vibrations of the truck trudging uphill lulled her to sleep, like a rhythmic verse of poetry. She dreamed one of her poems was set to music, and heard it sung over and over again in her mind as the truck ascended the mountain. With every meter of asphalt they travelled, she felt as though she were reaching closer and closer to the blazing sun, as though she might soon be able to raise her hand to the sky and clutch the ball of fire in her palm.

Leah and Tsila settled into an apartment on Alfasi Street at the very heart of Rehavia, surrounded by professors and colleagues from the Hebrew University. Leah missed the azure glimmers of the sea which she had previously been able to glimpse from her balcony, and the salty, humid air. She missed her faithful friends, but enjoyed the architecture of Jerusalem, and the greenery between the stone buildings. She found refuge in her books and papers, making steady progress on her translation of Tolstoy, as she prepared the lectures for her first semester at the Hebrew University.

She was shocked to find a full auditorium on her first day. *Did Jerusalemites recognize her name after all? Would her lectures live up to their expectations?*

Heart pounding, Leah approached the podium and delivered her lecture with a trembling voice. She could not tell whether the students were captivated by her words, or if they could even understand her Russian-inflected Hebrew.

Leah went home exhausted, grateful that her mother served her a hot dinner to soothe her stomach and warm her soul.

To relax after a long day of lecturing, Leah sat at the kitchen table, and, picking up pen and paper, sketched the characters for her next children's book. She sometimes wondered how she could possibly know what would be compelling for the children of Israel, when she had no children of her own, nor even any nieces or nephews, but her books were, somehow, always well received.

Before she had taken up her position at the Hebrew University, her fellow poets in Tel Aviv had warned her that she wouldn't find the time to write amid the constant pressure of preparing lectures. How right they were! She didn't think anything could ever prevent her from writing, as the need to be an artist, to create, burned in her soul. But preparing lectures was demanding, and by the time she returned home after lecturing all day, she was so exhausted that she could not muster the energy to keep on working. At first, she thought about waking up early and writing at six in the morning, but the muse never visited before she'd had her first cup of coffee and her first smoke, and by then it was time to get dressed and leave. What a pity that the Mount Scopus campus had been cut off from the rest of Jerusalem in a bloody attack on a convoy during the War of Independence; apparently the view from there of Temple Mount was breathtaking. She appreciated the walk through the shaded streets, often surprised by a new bud emerging from beneath a rock along the way. On occasions such as these, she'd be moved to pause and jot down a verse or two in her notebook, even if it meant arriving a few minutes late at Terra Sancta College. *If only I can inspire the younger generation, I will have done my part.*

Walking the corridors of the Literature Department one day, an elderly man who introduced himself as Professor Theodore Eckhart stopped Leah mid-stride.

"You're Leah Goldberg, aren't you?"

"Yes, I am."

"I've read all your books. Would you like to join me this evening for a literary soirée at Ticho House? I think you'd like Anna very much."

—

Leah noticed how graciously Anna greeted all her guests at the door of the mansion, but she couldn't help feel that she wasn't dressed smartly enough, and that her accent wasn't quite right. Leah knew that Anna took pride in the lushness of her garden and in her appearance, and expected her guests to live up to the same standards of personal grooming, though it was far from the norm in dusty Jerusalem. Though Anna seemed proud of her ever-expanding literary circle and welcomed new members every month, she kept it small and exclusive, clearly enjoying her position at the heart of Jerusalem's intelligentsia. As a professor, Leah would undoubtedly be a worthy addition.

Leah took a seat next to the colleague who had invited her to join the salon. To assuage her nerves, she reached into her purse and pulled out a cigarette and a matchbox. Raising the cigarette to her lips, she was about to strike a match, when she sensed those sitting around her shuffling in their seats.

"Excuse me, but the hostess does not permit smoking at these gatherings," informed the woman sitting in front of her, as she turned to face Leah. "The smoke would damage Anna's paintings."

Leah returned the unused cigarette to its case, but continued clasping her hands together, nervously intertwining and unlacing her fingers as she looked up at the row of paintings on the wall. She wondered how Anna found the time to produce so many new paintings each month, alongside her nursing responsibilities in her husband's ophthalmic clinic, and managing the household staff to maintain such a spotless residence.

Leah appreciated Anna's style and technique, and wished she could paint like her and accompany her children's books with illustrations of her own, rather than always submitting to the interpretation of other illustrators. Even the great Shmuel Katz had misrepresented the nightingale as a female bird in her children's book *A Flat to Let*. Maybe Anna would teach her to paint someday ...

Leah's contemplation of the paintings was interrupted by the woman's persistent voice. "Although it is a little-known fact as yet, as a physician I can tell you that smoking is detrimental to your health," the woman asserted. "I am Doctor Helena Kagan, by the way."

"Pleased to make your acquaintance," mumbled Leah under her breath.

"It will almost certainly shorten your life, as tobacco is one of the leading causes of cancer," another voice chipped in. "You have so much talent, so much to contribute, what a pity to cut your life short and subject yourself to such an excruciating death."

"I've never asked for anything more than to write one significant literary work," responded Leah. "Even if smoking turns out to be harmful, I've already accomplished everything I've set out to do. The potential for literary creation is, of course, endless, but I must be content with what I've accomplished so far, not knowing if I'll ever be able to reproduce my initial success."

A young man in a top hat sitting across from her suddenly spoke up: "Tell me, Ms. Goldberg, why are all your poems about the same subject—the torments of unrequited love? Why are they nothing but a variation on a theme?"

All I've ever hoped for, thought Leah, *my one wish, that has not yet been fulfilled, is to experience the fullness of love. Is it any wonder that my poems all harp on the same subject? What is life without an experience of love?*

"I am Nahman Zelikovitch, by the way," the man introduced himself, extending his hand to shake hers. "Not to be confused with Haim Nahman Bialik." Leah thought he seemed like a nice enough fellow, but she reciprocated the handshake reluctantly. Despite his youth, he seemed to fit right in with the salon members of German origin.

"I have no doubt you'll have seen my work in the trendiest journals," he continued. "I'll have you know that my poems constitute true poetry. You'll see, Leah Goldberg, the next phase of Hebrew poetry will be shaped by me."

Despite his arrogance, her heart had fluttered at his mention of unrequited love. For the fleetest moment she had hoped that, perhaps, he would be the one with whom she was intended to experience the fullness of love. But that was clearly not to be.

"No doubt," responded Leah, lowering her eyes to the interlaced hands cradled in her lap. She had, in fact, recently seen his name in one of the literary journals she read on a regular basis, but truth be told, hadn't been impressed. She found his poetry pretentious, though he advocated the use of simple language and free verse.

After a number of readings, which Leah barely followed, so agitated was she by Nahman's comments, Anna finally called on her to present her translation of Ibsen's plays. Few people knew it, but the theater had been Leah's first love. From a young age, she'd harbored a secret desire to become a stage actress; ever since that enchanted day as a child, when her mother had taken her to see a production at Kovno's splendid theater. She'd been mesmerized by the magic of the play, though the moral struck her as Communist propaganda. She'd dreamt of conquering the stage ever since.

As a student in Berlin, she'd attended many classical and experimental performances. She'd thought that an actress's life would be glamorous, but also knew the closest she'd ever get to a life on the stage was as a translator of plays. She was too timid to expose herself in front of an audience of hundreds.

Over the years, she'd earned recognition as a writer; in fact, her ticket to the Land of Israel, at a time when the number of Jewish immigrants was strictly restricted by the British, was acquired for her by Avraham Shlonsky, leader of the *Yahdav* (Together) literary circle. She had been hailed as the newest talent of the group, the only woman among them, and Shlonsky even published her first book, *Rings of Smoke*. She remembered her ecstasy upon first holding the book in her hands as she disembarked from the ship on the shores of Tel Aviv, an ecstasy that would soon turn into horror when she noticed the errors scattered throughout the book. She couldn't help but think that a poet's responsibility for their published work was greater even than to their children, as poems could potentially reach and influence thousands of people.

When she agreed to come along to the Ticho salon that evening, she'd hoped to meet one of Israel's leading actresses, who would appreciate her translation of Ibsen's *Doll's House*, but as far as she could tell, there weren't any actors in attendance; perhaps they were all occupied with rehearsals that day, or perhaps Anna did not consider their art to be on par with painting and literature.

As Leah read the opening pages, she felt as though she were embodying Nora's voice in her disappointment with domestic life.

That's it, she thought. *She could translate plays, present them at the Ticho salon as staged readings, and fulfil her theatrical aspirations by taking on a leading woman's role.*

As her reading came to an end, a strong male voice rose from the audience:

"Why should we be a translated nation? It is nothing but a disaster, this movement to translate classical literature into Hebrew. We are only interested in original works here."

The man in the elegant suit introduced himself as Avraham Yitzhak Kariv. He believed he was speaking on behalf of all the People of Israel.

Leah cringed, her efforts repudiated.

After giving up on Nahman Zelikovitch, Leah had thought that Kariv—with his chic elegance—might be the one for her, but he, too, had disappointed. She did believe that original Hebrew literature was of utmost importance. Ever since she was a girl, her soul had yearned to compose original Hebrew verse. She had, long ago, confided in her diary that, for her, to write, but not in Hebrew, would be just as painful as not writing at all. So why was she, of all people, scapegoated as a representative of those who wished to create a translated nation? Wasn't her substantial corpus of Hebrew prose and poetry evidence enough of her commitment to original Hebrew literature? She believed that in order to compose literature in any language, one had to familiarize themselves with the world's great books, and that was her role as a translator, to make those works accessible to her fellow Israelis—not to replace original Hebrew literature.

"Who needs all these Balzacs and Stendhals?" exclaimed Kariv. *How ironic*, thought Leah, *as he himself is a renowned translator.*

How very strange, she pondered. She had, after all, been invited to join the salon as a translator and scholar of Russian literature and, as far as she could tell, most members of the salon were nostalgic for the culture of Europe they'd left behind. In Vienna, where Anna had first studied art, Jugendstil had thrived and had been known in some circles as the Jewish style; Jewish writers, artists, and philosophers had always had a marked influence on German culture. Were those among them who had chosen to immigrate to Palestine, now Israel, regretful that their name would only ever be known in this small provincial town and not in the vastness of European civilization? The Jewish artists and intellectuals of Vienna and Berlin had been the first to go—a threat to the Nazi regime apparently—the first to be rounded up and shipped off to their deaths in cattle carts. It was here in Jerusalem that Jewish culture would finally flourish, making a significant contribution to world culture.

But could modern Hebrew literature really be created in a vacuum? Modern Hebrew was a relatively new language—it needed a literary tradition on which to base itself. S. Y. Agnon's language was grounded in the Torah and Mishnah, but his oeuvre was unique and didn't really appeal to the younger generation.

I'd like my poems to be read by people of all ages and backgrounds, thought Leah, *not just those who grew up within the confines of European yeshivas. I would like young lovers to pick up my books and be moved by my verses—recite them to each other—a new language of love befitting the current day. I have no choice but to rely on modern European poetry; I know of no other model, just as in her painting, Anna is indebted to the precision of the Viennese aesthetic. That's where she got her artistic training—she can't all of a sudden uproot herself from Europe to the Middle East and unlearn everything she'd learned before.*

As for me, reflected Leah, *though I was born in Germany, the borders have become so fluid since the War that I was influenced by Russian literature and culture. I am aware that the German intellectuals here consider me to be less sophisticated than they, even though Russian literature ranks among the world's greatest cultural achievements.* She was, nonetheless, glad to have been invited to join the salon—a small, hidden remnant of Europe within this Middle Eastern city—and engage once again in serious conversation about poetry and aesthetics.

Leah often thought of Anna as a painterly parallel, a pioneering woman artist who had made a name for herself even before the State's establishment. She had, of course, heard of her while still living in Tel Aviv, when her paintings were exhibited there, and the entire artistic community of the young city flocked to see her work. Her style had clearly evolved over the years, and Leah had been inspired by her paintings, seeing ancient Jerusalem through a new lens.

Leah couldn't suppress the thought that Anna's accomplishments were doubly impressive given the fact that she devoted the majority of her waking hours to assisting her husband in his ophthalmology clinic and playing hostess. *Maybe it's a good thing I never married,* she thought—not only for fear of transmitting her father's mental illness, but also knowing that her husband's career would surely have taken precedence over her own art. She was fortunate to have her mother doing all the cooking and cleaning for her, so she could concentrate on her writing.

—

Leah and Tsila boarded bus 405 to Tel Aviv from Jerusalem's central station. Leah often travelled that route, enjoying the lull of the ride, the rhythm of the motion. It was still early and, though it was going to be a hot day, Leah and Tsila were dressed in gray tweed suits, pearl earrings and necklaces, feathered cloche hats—ready for that night's première of Ibsen's *Doll's House* translated by Leah.

The elegant women sitting on either side of them at the Tel Aviv theater wore strapless ball gowns in bright colors, their bosoms tightly clad in corsets. They gazed deploringly at Leah's and Tsila's gray tweeds. Leah knew that such mono-chromatic suits with plain, knee-length skirts were all the rage in Europe, had become classic women's wear, ever since Coco Chanel had introduced them as the garments of liber-ated women in the world's fashion capital, Paris.

She would finally have the opportunity to get as close as possible to the stage, but once again in the company of her mother, while all the other attendees had come as couples, arms entwined. Only she had no man to escort her. No matter. They had front row seats and she could see up the lead actress's nostrils as she played the part of Nora, could see the beads of perspiration forming on her forehead under the heat of the spotlights—but, best of all, the words coming out of her painted lips were Leah's. She had brought this pinnacle of Modernist drama to life in Hebrew; knew every line of it by heart.

The theater itself was a minimalist utilitarian structure with a plain wooden stage, so unlike the magnificent theater she had so often frequented as a doctoral student in Berlin, where the ceiling was ornate, with gold leaf molding. How she had envied all those young women, undoubtedly less accomplished than herself (though she was, admittedly, less attractive), who were accompanied by tall, handsome young men. She wondered now, looking back, how many of those young men she'd seen at the Berlin theater had gone on to join the Nazis and led her fellow Jews to their deaths. On the other hand, it was interesting that a former Hitler Youth member had followed her Jewish sweetheart to Israel after the war and was now making a name for herself on the Tel Aviv stage.

Perhaps her attraction to lecturing stemmed from her fascination with the theater, the closest she would ever get to the glamor of an actor's life. Hundreds of students would clamor into the auditorium at Terra Sancta College to listen to her at the podium, some even sitting in the stairwell—a captive audience. She'd be so absorbed in the day's text that she'd embody the spirit of the characters, their voices rising from her throat, as though she were a stage actress. Hundreds of attentive sets of eyes would be directed at her as she improvised free translations of the passages she'd learned by heart, savoring the weight of the Hebrew words on her lips.

Sometimes a new poem would come to her as she took the scenic route through the fields of the Valley of the Cross on her way home to 16 Alfasi Street, after lecturing all day. She would come out of the packed lecture hall into the dusk, the sun just starting to set, and would take a detour across the fields, wildflowers sprouting on either side of the path, as the words of the European writer she had taught that day—Dostoyevsky, Tolstoy—resonated in her mind as new Hebrew verses formed. Though she was racing against the setting sun, afraid to be caught alone in the darkness of the vast valley, she would stop to jot down the words in her notebook. The pacing of her steps against the soft grass somehow became immortalized in the meter of her poems.

Eclipse of the Stars

We are caught / Like butterflies by the sentries of your yearning
                                                    —Nelly Sachs

Nelly's heart fluttered as she opened the thin envelope from Paris and pulled out Paul's letter. As always, the message was short but heartfelt—he was about to embark on a trip to Israel. Did she care to join?

Nelly closed her eyes and imagined Israel, about which she'd written several poems. Would she finally get to see it with her own eyes?

It was, in fact, the perfect time to make the trip. Jerusalem had just been unified, and her mother was no longer alive, so there was no need for her to stay at home, there was no one requiring her care.

What if she did see it with her own eyes—would it destroy her fantasy? Would she have to scrap the poems she'd written about it, never having seen it?

Land of Israel,
chosen starry place
for the celestial kiss!

Did she even have the strength to climb onto an airplane and make the cross-European flight to the Middle East? How cumbersome—the very thought of packing her suitcase exhausted her.

She'd heard that there was a group of German artists and writers active in Jerusalem and was curious to meet them— they'd probably give her a hero's reception if she came for a visit.

She would like to reconnect with S. Y. Agnon, whom she'd only met briefly the previous year, when he arrived in Stockholm to receive the Nobel Prize in Literature, which they had shared. He had then been on her territory; she could now reciprocate and go to his. Seeing Jerusalem through the eyes of Shmuel Yosef Agnon would be nothing less than spectacular; of that she was quite certain.

Nelly momentarily raised her eyes from Paul's letter and looked out the window above her writing desk. A yellow butterfly fluttered from rose to rose in the garden just outside her window. *The butterfly must be a sign*, she thought, *a sign of the Hebrew spirit*.

She sat down in her chair, pulled out a fresh sheet of paper, dipped her fountain pen in ink, and composed her response to Paul's letter. Succinct, but enthusiastic.

Setting down her pen, she raised her eyes again to look out the window—the yellow butterfly fluttering from flower to flower appeared to be performing a dance, moving rhythmically, with grace. She followed it with her eyes, her torso bouncing in her chair to the rhythm of the music she imagined accompanying the butterfly's dance. The melody started playing itself in her head, and she remembered dancing to that music as a fourteen-year-old girl, when her ambition had been to become a famous dancer.

As a teenager, her arms stretched over her head, pirouetting—never once growing dizzy—throwing her leg up in the air in an arabesque, then performing a jump and landing gracefully on both feet on the wooden stage, had filled her with joy. The applause overwhelmed her, and she ran to the wing, relieved that the performance was over. Soon after, she realized she was far too shy to pursue a life on the stage and turned her energies to writing poetry. The rhythm of her verses continued to align with the music, the words springing, whirling, and falling down again as she caught her breath, declaiming themselves with the grace of a dancer.

When she was just starting off as a poet, an older poet had told her that writing should be like a dance: it should look effortless to the readers. Just as a ballerina does not exhale loudly before leaping, so too should good writing be graceful, smoothly rolling off the reader's tongue.

She sometimes missed that life—the spotlights, the stage—but knew that the life of the reclusive poetess suited her far better, especially living as she had for thirty years in a foreign land. Though dance may be a universal language, the only language she could write in was German, her mother tongue, though it was foreign to the ears of her adopted compatriots. She could not express herself, nor the plight of her people, in any other language, and dance seemed too joyful, too irreverent, to convey the atrocities her people had experienced in her homeland. Not to mention that she was already too old to appear on stage, her body not nearly as agile as it had been in her youth, her bones brittle.

But was Germany her homeland? Wasn't her true homeland a place she'd never seen? Maybe she'd finally have the opportunity to see it with her own eyes, that ancient land for which her people had yearned for millennia. There was no better time for it as Jerusalem, the holiest city of all, had just been reunited under Jewish sovereignty—nothing less than a modern-day miracle.

Her shoulders hunched over the paper, the wrinkles on her face growing more defined as she composed her response, squinting to see the letters. She would finally get to see the Land of Israel, after imagining it for seventy odd years. But what if she was disappointed, if the reality didn't live up to her expectations? What if her poems proved to be no longer relevant? Would she have to retract them? Would she then have to return the Nobel Prize, awarded to her on the basis of those poems? Agnon would certainly be pleased to be declared sole recipient. What if the ground, stones, and trees of the Holy Land were so marvelous that she could never write another poem—that her voice would be forever silenced, overwhelmed by the beauty of God's beloved city, starkly aware that her words could never live up to those standards of beauty? Didn't the Talmud state that Jerusalem took nine out of ten measures of the world's beauty? She did not doubt it was true.

She was willing to take the risk, though, having already accomplished her corpus of work, an oeuvre she could be proud of. Most importantly, however, it had helped her survive in exile, had allowed her to express her people's sorrow. It was poetry that had saved her life, and that enabled her to memorialize the lives of those who had perished.

Having sealed the envelope, Nelly hurried to hand it over to her secretary to take to the post office. Ever since she had received the Prize, even though it was only half the usual sum as she had shared it with Agnon, she was able to afford a secretary, who also served as a companion of sorts—helping alleviate her loneliness since her mother's death. If there was one thing she regretted, it was that her mother hadn't lived to see her receiving the Nobel Prize, walking up to the podium at the palace in Stockholm to shake His Majesty's hand and deliver her brief acceptance speech.

Her mother had been her only companion since they'd escaped Nazi Germany, and they'd taken care of each other in their darkest moments. Her mother would have been proud to see that Nelly's efforts had paid off, that she'd finally been recognized for her contribution to the literary canon and to the Jewish People.

For years, she'd been on her own, friendless, reclusive. Perhaps it would do her good to travel to Israel with her pen pal, Paul Celan, enjoy his camaraderie, his wit, if only for a week or two.

When the secretary returned from the post office, she asked him to arrange for a plane ticket for her to Israel, departing in two weeks' time. She'd hardly ever been on an airplane and was afraid of traveling by air, but it would save her the time and the seasickness that inevitably accompanied boat rides. It was, apparently, miraculous technology—rising up into the air like a bird, soaring above the clouds, and then descending again and landing on foreign soil in a matter of hours. Some people absolutely swore by it.

She rose from her desk and asked her secretary to bring her the small leather suitcase from the storage room—the same one with which she had fled Germany and crossed the Baltic Sea in 1940, to find refuge in Sweden, with the help of Selma Lagerlöf, one of her favorite writers. Then, too, literature had been her salvation. It was the only suitcase she'd been permitted to take out of Germany and, though it was small, it had sufficed to contain her important belongings. She'd had no reason to procure another piece of luggage since, as she hadn't gone anywhere.

Once retrieved from storage, Nelly began filling the suitcase herself. It was delicate, over thirty years old, and threatening to crumble. She wouldn't let anybody else handle it, nor did she want her secretary to touch her few prized personal items. She was too private a person to display her dirty—or even her clean—laundry.

Looking through her closet for the garments that would be most suitable for the Mediterranean sun, her hands shook, drawing a melody from the thin metal hangers vibrating against the wooden rod. She examined the lines on the back of her hands, testimony to decades of hardship.

Dressed in her beige suit—she couldn't possibly meet a fellow Nobel laureate in a housedress, nor could she step on sacred ground in anything undignified—her suitcase was finally ready and sealed, and she placed it by the front door.

Nelly swallowed two valerian pills before embarking.

—

Beads of perspiration formed on Nelly's forehead as she stepped off the plane and down the stairs. She set her foot down on the sacred earth just outside Tel Aviv. Not only was it hot, it was humid. Even the hottest days in Stockholm couldn't compare to this oppressive heat.

She felt proud as the clerk stamped her passport with the emblem of the *menorah* surrounded by olive branches and the words State of Israel below—her dream had finally become a reality and she had made it there in one piece.

It was an emotional moment as she met her pen pal in person for the first time. His bald head shining and his eyes glimmering, Paul waited for her in the meet and greet area.

Their first destination was a pilgrimage to the Mount of Olives, to pay homage at the grave of a fellow German-Jewish poetess, Else Lasker-Schüler, whose Expressionist poetry also spoke of the Land of Israel as God's beloved, and of the People of Israel as her own. Though her poetry had won the Kleist Prize in 1932, she was chased out of Germany soon after and made her way to Palestine—but as Nelly feared, earthly Jerusalem had disappointed her, hadn't lived up to the heavenly Jerusalem of her imagination, and she had died, heartbroken, in 1945.

Now that Jerusalem had been unified, it was possible for her to reach the Mount of Olives, having previously been cut off from Western Jerusalem for many years. If she'd come just a few months prior, a stone barrier would have stood in her way. Still, her heart was pounding as she sat next to Paul in the black car, absorbing the heat of the blazing sun, even though the windows had been rolled all the way down.

When the car came to a stop, Paul extended his hand to help Nelly out. Unstable on her feet, her voice shook as she stood by Else's grave, reading aloud poems in German from her predecessor's last collection, *My Blue Piano*, launched years ago at Ticho House, Nelly's next destination. The German words caught in her throat. Not only were Else's words moving, but Nelly had hardly spoken German since her mother's death—in Stockholm, she used Swedish to communicate with the few people she employed and saw on an occasional basis. Though German was her mother tongue and the language of her poetry, she knew that, to the ears of the *sabras*, there must be a dissonance. Though biblical Hebrew was their ancestral tongue, it was only in German that she and Paul and Else had been able to give expression to the plight of their people in the Holocaust, when they'd been victimized for no reason other than their religion and race. But now the People of Israel were considered heroic, as they had vanquished several Arab armies in just six days and had recaptured significant masses of the land for which the Jews had yearned for millennia. The photograph of the three officers who had liberated the Old City of Jerusalem, kissing the ancient stones of the Western Wall, was on display everywhere she went—from the airport, to restaurants, and cultural centers. If that wasn't a modern-day miracle, a cause for amazement, she didn't know what was. For the first time in her life she felt safe, with no need to conceal her faith. After reciting Else's poems, she read one of her own poems to her:

"The voices of the dead
Speak through reed pipes of seclusion."

She'd been inspired by Else's poetry when she'd written it. As she had only started writing seriously after her arrival in Sweden, Else never knew what a great influence she'd had on her, how much her poetry resonated with her, and how much she'd inspired her. Perhaps she now watched from above, gratified by the poetic tribute.

Nelly remembered seeing Else in the cafés of Berlin, performing her poetry like the prince(ss) she believed herself to be. Nelly had been young then and admired Else for her talent and courage. She'd never imagined at that time that she, too, would gain fame for her poetry, or that anyone would care about or empathize with the Jewish victims to whom she sought to give a voice. But they had, and had even honored her for it, and she'd now come to express her thanks to Else, who had been her poetic mentor and spiritual guide, had shown her the way, had demonstrated what power words could have.

She'd been drawn to Else because of her love of dance. Though Else was first and foremost a poet and a painter, she was also a performer, climbing onto a table at the Romanisches Café as though it were a stage. Nelly would never have had the courage to do so, she was too meek, too ladylike, but she finally found her voice as a poet after her emigration. She was indebted to Else, couldn't have done it without her—wouldn't have known it was legitimate to write about the suffering of their people. She was glad to have the opportunity to pay homage at her grave in the world's oldest cemetery. It takes courage to be a poet, and even more so to be a poetess, and to continue writing in German, the language of the oppressors, on foreign soil. It was nothing short of a miracle that her own poetry had been published and recognized for its literary merit—a cry on behalf of her people, protesting the innumerable injustices to which they'd been subjected.

Standing there at Else's gravesite, Nelly wondered who would stand at her own grave. She knew she was nearing the end of her life and had no children of her own. The majority of her readers were in Germany. Sweden had been good to her, had treated her well, and Stockholm would henceforth be her only home.

A yellow butterfly fluttered around Else's grave. Nelly stuck her finger out as a perch. Was it Else's spirit descending from the heavens to listen to Nelly's praise?

Else had been labeled a "degenerate" artist and that entire group had fallen apart. Nelly had never belonged to a group of artists, and she was apprehensive about joining the Ticho House salon that evening.

—

Nelly put on her fanciest gown, silk with a modest lace collar, the same she'd worn to the Nobel Prize ceremony. Even Paul dressed in a suit and tie for the occasion. She was to be the guest of honor at that evening's gathering. She hardly ever dressed up, hardly ever had occasion to do so, but here she was now, world-famous, a celebrity among the group of German writers and artists living in Jerusalem.

She did not doubt that Anna and her staff had worked hard, had outdone themselves to impress her with the reception they'd prepared. Still, Nelly felt anxious. She wasn't used to being the center of attention, and she'd have to converse with Agnon again, who would be sharing the spotlight. Though she respected him as a writer, he had made her feel uneasy when she'd met him briefly in Stockholm, speaking to her in a condescending manner, unhappy to share the stage with a woman, as though her poetry could never measure up to the prolificity of his prose. He addressed her with arrogance, talking down to her, rather than conversing with a worthy equal, unwilling to acknowledge that she, too, was promoting the Jewish spirit through her poetic oeuvre. It was as though by sharing the prize with her, it detracted from his immense accomplishment, meant that his work was less worthy than that of previous, solo recipients.

Agnon was the only one who showed up at Ticho House that evening not wearing a suit. He stood out in his yarmulke, checked shirt, and khaki pants as he leaned against the furniture. Anna, the hostess, was gracious as always, and all of the guests standing in the entrance hall waiting to greet Nelly looked at her with admiration, except for Agnon, who remained cold and distant all night.

"You continue to give voice to the victims, rather than to our heroes, who established the State and have won miraculous victories over many Arab armies," accused Agnon. Challenging her about her poetry, he inquired: "How can you continue writing in German after the Germans destroyed our people?"

Paul immediately came to her defense, like a knight in shining armor: "A poet can only write in his or her mother tongue."

"But Hebrew has always been our people's ancestral language," persisted Agnon.

"And, yet, your own Hebrew, Shmuel Yosef, is unlike anybody else's. You've created a syntax of your very own," chimed in Leah Goldberg.

Ignoring Leah's remark and turning to Nelly, Agnon continued his tirade: "When the Nobel committee stated that we'd both contributed to the literature of the Jewish People, how could they possibly compare my output—thousands of densely written pages—to your few thin volumes, collections of concise poems, some of them blank other than the title?"

"I'll have you know that the economy of words and distillation of poetry is sometimes worth a thousand words," answered Nelly.

His torso hefty and his neck bent, Agnon pulled out a thin volume of Nelly's poetry from the pocket of his khaki pants. Flipping through the pages, he stopped at the header, "Eclipse of the Stars," followed by a dedication "In Memory of My Father." Nelly flinched as though her own spine were being overextended as he opened up the book, waving it in the air for everyone to see the blank page.

"And you call this a poem?" he asked with a derisive smile. "Aren't you ashamed of selling a book with blank pages in it, trying to pass it off as poetry?"

"That's just the dedication," responded Nelly in a near whisper. "But silence is sometimes the only appropriate mode of expression."

"It must have been a blow to his ego to share the Prize with a woman," remarked Leah. "Don't take it personally."

"I don't," agreed Nelly. "I don't seek anyone's approval. I write neither for acclaim nor fame. I write because I must. My mission has always been to give voice to the victims of the Holocaust, and it is to them that I remain true."

"You are a true poet," asserted Anna.

"Thank you, Anna, that means a lot to me and thank you for this lovely gathering." Nelly demurely bowed her neck.

"You do us honor with your presence," responded Anna. "Don't you worry, Nelly, some people have tried to dismiss my paintings as nothing but a feminine pastime. But I persisted and proved them all wrong. The exhibitions and prizes speak for themselves—as do your publications and the Nobel Prize—there is no greater recognition than that. A man's ego is extremely delicate, you know."

"I can't say I've ever known any man intimately, but I can only imagine. Paul is the closest male companion I've ever had, and I couldn't imagine a gentler, more kindred spirit. But he is married, you know. At the end of the day, my books are my children, my only legacy."

"Not a single day goes by that I don't miss my dear departed Albert," said Anna, "but even though we were blessed with close to five blissful decades together, only my paintings will survive me." Turning to Agnon, she continued: "I remain eternally grateful to you, Shmuel Yosef, for speaking so beautifully at Albert's sixtieth birthday. Why can't you speak to Nelly in the same spirit today?"

"How could they possibly regard us as equals?" Agnon responded, fuming. "Anyone can see that my work is far superior; you need only ask the opinion of any literary scholar in the room, some of whom never even heard Ms. Sachs's name until the Nobel Committee's announcement."

"Why don't you admit it, Shmuel Yosef, you are simply infuriated you had to share the prize with a woman. Tell us the truth, is that what's bothering you?" asked Leah.

"No, of course not," he stammered, "women dabble in poetry all the time; it doesn't make them great writers of my caliber. Besides, I've never heard of anyone sharing the Nobel Prize in literature. In science or economics, sure, but not in literature. You were only on the Committee's radar, Nelly, because you happen to live in Sweden and your poems have been published in Swedish translation; otherwise, you'd still be an anonymous poet. If you'd fled to Palestine rather than Sweden with the rise of the Nazi regime, like other more courageous writers, you'd still be unknown today."

"I beg to differ," interjected Paul. "I myself have published Nelly's poems in international literary journals, and they were very well received."

"You offend the core spirit of this group by criticizing the fact that Nelly writes in German. Don't you know it was founded by German expatriates?" chided Anna. "We invited you to join us tonight to celebrate Nelly's accomplishments on the occasion of her visit to Israel. It is not every day that we have a Nobel laureate among us. Thank you for honoring us with your presence, Nelly, for making time for us on your brief visit."

"I am deeply honored by your hospitality," responded Nelly in a weak voice, barely above a whisper.

A tall dark woman rose from her seat and, placing a hand on Nelly's shoulder, whispered in her ear: "You look weary, Nelly, are you unwell? I'm Doctor Helena Kagan, let me know if I can be of any assistance."

Nelly acknowledged the offer with a nod of her head, feeling her skin growing paler and her legs weaker, until she could no longer stand and was forced to take a seat on the sofa. Beside her, Doctor Kagan stood strong and sturdy, though she, too, was clearly advanced in years.

To dispel the tension, Helena signaled to her husband, Emil, and he, right on cue, picked up his violin and performed a virtuosic solo.

All Nelly wanted was to leave, to return to her solitary existence in Sweden or, bury herself under the embroidered cushions arranged on the couches. She'd never got over her childish shyness that had kept her from pursuing a career as a dancer all those years ago. She was glad to have Paul at her side, giving her strength, though she knew he, too, was fragile on the inside, that he had been profoundly scarred by his own experiences in the forced labor camp. She sometimes felt as though the Jews who had spent those war years in Israel couldn't quite grasp the magnitude of the atrocities their fellow Jews had suffered in Europe, all on account of their being Jewish.

While Anna's paintings demonstrated the beauty of the Land—its flora, its people, its unique architecture—Nelly felt that only words, or sometimes even the absence of words, could give expression to the emptiness that had been left in Europe as a result of the Holocaust. She was sorry Agnon felt her work to be incomparable to his, but she hadn't taken up poetry to impress anyone. It was nothing but a survival mechanism. She had done her part, even if she never wrote another word.

Tired and weary, Nelly turned to Paul and whispered in his ear, "I'd like to go now." He held a hand out to her and accompanied her to the entrance, where they thanked Anna and bid her farewell under the arch of Jerusalem stone framing the doorway.

—

Back at their hotel, Paul escorted Nelly to her room and kissed her hand before she closed the door behind her, leaving him standing in the corridor.

She sat down, dizzy, in a chair, to avoid falling, and reached down to the hem of her dress—a dress she would have no further use for. Pulling the soft silk over her head, she examined the wrinkles lining her skin, like deep rows raked in the earth, her body marked by time, by sorrow.

Regardless of what Agnon thought, she knew she had done her part for the Jewish People, but she could write no more poems now that she had seen Jerusalem with her own eyes.

Resting her head on the pillow in her narrow bed, she slipped into a dazed slumber and, all through the night, was visited by a yellow butterfly fluttering around her head.

Butterfly
blessed night of all beings!
The weights of life and death
sink down with your wings
on the rose
which withers with the light ripening homewards.

Part III

Jerusalem and Beyond

2000s

Flower of Eden

Each morning at sunrise, when the call of the *muezzin* coincided with the ringing of church bells and the blowing of the *shofar* at the Western Wall, Adina opened the window of her stone house overlooking the Old City. On that late summer day, she pulled the curtains apart, opened the shutters, and breathed in the fresh air filled with the perfume of lavender and the appetizing smell of hyssop. The stones of the wall surrounding the city gleamed in the first rays of sunlight, and the blades of the windmill spun in the final breeze of the night. The only unpleasant sight was the pot of geraniums on her windowsill, whose leaves were turning a crisp yellow, scorched by the summer sun.

Adina forced herself to wake at dawn. She was spending the year as part of the artists' colony of Mishkenot Sha'ananim and wished to take advantage of each moment to observe the sights, listen to the sounds, smell the perfumes, meet the people, and explore the city; discover everything that made it unique and distinguished it from her native Chicago, where she had recently completed a degree in music performance, specializing in the violin.

At home, bored and uninspired, she had repeated and perfected the same pieces without advancing. She was sure that here she would finally find the thrill she needed to infuse Tchaikovsky's *Violin Concerto in D Major* with the feeling it required to sound like more than simply a chain of consecutive notes. Still, no matter how many hours she spent rehearsing, her fingers dispassionately slid up and down and across the strings of the instrument. She appreciated the deadline, the gathering of the colony's artists at the end of every month when each had fifteen minutes to present his or her most recent work.

Each morning at the very moment when Adina leaned out the window, a dark-haired, barefooted man smoking a pipe ran up the stairs near her house. One day, he stopped below her window, took his pipe out of his mouth, and said *"shalom"* in a soft voice. She lowered her gaze, but before she could respond he had already pursued his journey in a light, quick stride, whistling an oriental tune.

Adina smiled to herself, inhaling the fresh air. She was constantly amazed by the warmth of Jerusalem's inhabitants, and by their beauty. She considered the man handsome: dark skin, dark eyes, a tall, lean, muscular build. She clasped her hands together, stretched them above her head, and let them fall right over her heart.

As was her daily habit, Adina stationed herself on a stool by the open window and practiced her violin for two hours, until the cafés opened. After grabbing a latté and an omelet wrap, she'd take a walk around the city and would return home at noon, when the heat reached its peak. After a cold lunch and a quick nap, she'd return to her violin by the window. The evenings were devoted to outings to the cinema, theater, or concerts.

The following day the man reappeared, paused, and smiled. This time Adina was expecting him. She said "hello" and inquired about his health. The next day, a Friday, he did not come. Adina waited by her window for an hour, scanning the staircases at either end of the block, twirling strands of her long, wavy brown hair around her finger. Saturday went by with no sign of him, either. Adina was disappointed. She dutifully sat herself down by the window and tuned the violin, but jumped up whenever she heard footsteps outside. She did not see him among the groups of tourists and returned to her instrument.

On Sunday he reappeared, much to Adina's delight. She was watering the geraniums in a last attempt to save them. The man noticed her frown and glanced at the dying flowers. "Why don't you give them spring water instead of tap water," he suggested.

"I doubt it'll help. There are hardly any healthy petals left," she said with a shrug, putting the watering can down on the windowsill.

"Don't worry; tomorrow I'll bring you some special compost," he promised.

—

The following morning, he carried a plastic bag, out of which he pulled a glass jar filled to the rim with a chunky brown substance. "Mix it into the earth and the petals will grow red again," he advised her.

"Thank you," she said.

With a bow of his head, he was on his way. Only after he had disappeared among the houses did she turn to the geraniums and spoon the compost into the earth, careful not to break the roots.

The next day, on his way to work, the man examined the flowers.

"Is it fire of passion raining down doom?
Is it longing that makes rose flowers bloom?" he pondered.

"I beg your pardon?" Adina raised her eyebrow.

"I was just saying how beautiful the flowers look."

Adina nodded in agreement. The compost had begun to do its work.

Every morning as the man passed by her window, he stopped to admire the flowers. He would often describe them with poetic words, and it was only after several days that Adina realized he was actually praising her beauty. He would pause below her window, look up at Adina's face, think for an instant, and let a line of poetry roll from his tongue: *"A smile's paradise bloomed on her rose cheek."* Each day she anticipated his arrival and her heart fluttered whenever she spotted him from afar.

Adina knew many poets from around the world at the colony, but none made her feel as he did. They were arrogant and rational; he was simple, authentic, spontaneous, and passionate. While the other poets prided themselves on the complexity and opaqueness of their language, his compositions emerged directly from his heart. He was unlike anyone she had ever met: poor yet rich inside, an amateur yet more profound than the professionals.

On a particularly warm morning, a late autumn heat wave, the man reached Adina's house, his face flushed and his mouth so dry that he could barely pronounce the day's verse.

Adina rushed into the kitchen and filled a tall glass with cold water, ashamed that she had never thought of offering him anything to drink. She ran down the stairs, drops of water spraying in all directions, pulled out a plastic chair, and handed him the glass. He gulped down the contents even before collapsing into a seated position.

"If every divine gift were glorified
We would ever be in praise occupied." He kissed her hand.

"Please come in for some refreshments," she offered, without pulling her hand away.

"I can't, I'm on my way to work, but I'll gladly stop by in the afternoon, on my way home," he responded.

Adina spent the entire day preparing for his visit. She could not focus on her music and her violin remained silent. Adina collected her scores from the living room table, polished the bathroom mirror, and washed the floor. She even baked chocolate chip cookies. Closer to the time of his arrival, she straightened her hair, applied makeup, and sprayed perfume.

A few minutes before he was due to arrive, she brewed a pot of tea. According to the local custom, she poured boiling water over fresh peppermint, lemongrass, and sage leaves, sweetening the concoction with honey. Just as he knocked, she took two porcelain mugs and her favorite hand-embroidered napkins out of the cupboard.

Adina rushed to open the door, the china still rattling on the living room table. The aroma of tobacco and cologne filled the entrance hall. At eye level, he appeared even more impressive than from above. He had unfastened the top two buttons of his checked shirt, and the diagonal line formed by the collar defined his facial features. His white teeth gleamed against his dark skin as he smiled at her.

"Please, come in," she invited after a pause, extending her hand to him. The man took her hand, followed her inside, and sat down on the sofa next to her. For a few minutes, they just sat there, observing each other, smiling timidly, catching each other's eyes, and turning their heads away.

The man's eyes finally rested on the plate of cookies and Adina, following his gaze, pushed it closer into his reach and filled his glass. She watched as he dipped a biscuit into his tea, took a bite, and chewed with appetite.

"Delicious!" he said, reaching for a second.

Adina blushed, picked up a napkin, and leaned forward to wipe away the crumb that had fallen from his lip. She held the crumpled napkin in her hand as she poured tea into her own mug and finally found the courage to ask: "What's your name?"

"Call me Amir."

"Amir, Am-eer," she repeated, slowly rolling her tongue against her palate. "What a beautiful name! What does it mean?"

"In Hebrew it means 'apex' and in Arabic it means 'prince'."

"It suits you perfectly. Where are you from? What do you do?"

"I live across the valley in the Old City," he pointed out the open window. "I'm an architect, currently designing the towers for Emek Refaim, but at heart, I am a poet, just like you."

"You are a much better poet than me. I'm not a poet at all," she replied. "I just play the violin."

"I've heard you playing on my way home from work." Adina imagined him sitting on the stone steps or leaning against the outer wall of the house in order to catch his breath, tapping his foot to the rhythm. "Only a poet could play like that."

Adina smiled and her cheeks reddened. She had never considered herself a poet, only an interpreter of other people's compositions; but perhaps seeing him had affected her, had already altered her performance in some subtle way she herself could not discern.

"Would you recite some more of your poetry for me?" she asked.

He put his mug down and cleared his throat. "I don't usually share my poems with anyone, but you're special."

"They thought a heart's wound a bed of rose blooms
They thought bloody streams were fallen red blooms."

Adina enjoyed his soft voice, punctuated with a guttural accent. As she contemplated the elaborate Hebrew words she had just heard, he consulted his watch and startled her by rising from the sofa and heading to the door. "I'm sorry, but I must get home now. I have to make dinner for my ailing parents and bathe them." Before leaving, he kissed Adina's cheek and promised to return the following day.

He winked at her when he went by her window the next morning and she anticipated his arrival all day long. In the afternoon they sat together for an hour, watching the sunset from her rooftop as he recited poetry and she played the violin.

Adina found herself thinking more and more of Amir as she practiced. She quivered as the bow caressed the strings of the instrument, as though his fingers were gliding over her shoulder. She was motivated to remain at the violin longer than usual and rehearsed her piece with greater fervor.

Amir complimented her on her progress. He, in turn, would give her a one-line preview each morning on his way to work and the full poem in the afternoon, dealing with love, beauty or the nature of art. She was impressed with his ability to come up with an original poem every single day, as well as with his prodigious memory.

The following Friday, Adina was again distraught by Amir's absence. *He must devote his day off work to caring for his parents,* she thought. But she was cheered by the geraniums on her windowsill. They had regained their color, new leaves were growing, and buds were unfurling.

The two days without Amir were difficult for Adina. She could not stop thinking of him, but she couldn't even call him and talk on the phone, because she knew neither his number nor his full name. To distract herself, she practiced scales. After half an hour of false notes and unstable tempo, she gave up, ran out of her house, down the stairs into the valley, across the road, up the hill along the dirt path, past the Armenian monastery, and through Zion Gate into the Jewish Quarter of the Old City.

She hoped to encounter Amir; perhaps he'd see her walking by his window and come out to meet her. Losing herself in the narrow alleyways, she passed crowds of men in white shirts and woven yarmulkes or black hats returning home to their families from Shabbat morning services, their *talitot* still draped over their shoulders, the fringed edges swaying in the breeze. She also saw the occasional young couple, walking as close to each other as they could without touching. The women wore multicolored headscarves and seamless white tops that stretched over their round bellies; they seemed so happy, so tranquil, so light, despite the added weight. She noticed little children running ahead of their parents, chasing each other, their jackets slipping off one shoulder, ties loosened and shoelaces undone. Those even younger held their fathers' hands, trying to keep up or hiding from older children behind their legs. Those not yet able to walk were carried by their parents, held in a tight embrace.

Adina imagined herself as Amir's wife, walking along these same streets with him, the sunlight refracted from the Jerusalem stone reflected against his face. She had never considered permanently settling in Israel, let alone in Jerusalem's Old City, but now the idea appealed to her. The more distance she covered, the more she found to like about the Old City: its stone walls, eclectic architecture, secret paths, and hidden gardens.

She wandered until the heat made her dizzy and the scent of fresh *challah* reminded her she hadn't yet eaten that day. When she couldn't find an open kiosk or grocer in the Jewish Quarter, she debated whether to venture into the Arab *suk*, but didn't feel secure doing so, a Jewish woman alone, knowing neither the language nor the customs. She went back across the valley to her home.

——

Amir reappeared on Sunday and sat with her for an hour in the afternoon. To make up for the two days he had missed, he brought her a green herbal ball that he dropped into the teapot. Together, cheek to cheek, his rough, prickly stubble against her soft skin, they stared at the ball through the clear glass and watched as it slowly swelled, expanded, and unfurled. First, a layer of stringy leaves dropped and encircled the thick green core like a Hawaiian grass skirt; then a fluffy red pompon emerged on top.

"It's called Flower of Eden," he informed her. "It infuses the tea with an aroma like rosewater, only sweeter."

After a few sips, they turned to each other and spent the rest of the hour with interlocked lips, savoring the Flower of Eden's sweetness. Adina felt so comfortable in his strong, muscular arms and did not want to let go. But no matter how much she implored him to stay and have dinner with her, he refused, insisting that he had to be home by six.

After his departure, she drained the unfinished teapot, dried the red flower, and placed it on top of the fruit bowl in the center of her living room table. He had proven himself to be a poet even in his most mundane actions. She pitied him; such a talented man supervising construction sites so he could support his dying parents, when he should be writing poetry full-time.

—

She invited him to join her at the monthly artists' assembly. When they entered the Conference Hall, they headed straight for the loveseat. David, an Australian painter, who was already sitting there, made way for them before they passed the threshold. They held hands for the duration of the session. Adina played Tchaikovsky's *Violin Concerto in D Major* better than she ever had before, and Amir clapped loudest after her performance.

At the end of the evening, Adina introduced Amir. "He's a poet, a native Jerusalemite, who writes in Hebrew. If no one objects to staying another five minutes, he'll recite a poem or two for us."

The host nodded his approval. Amir stood and advanced to the podium. He looked striking in the new navy-blue suit and leather shoes Adina had bought him for the occasion.

"I'll recite an excerpt of the poem 'On the Nature of Poethood',"he announced. Amir stood tall and delivered his poem in a resonant voice:

"To say poet is to say man of heart
A tolerant man and gentle of heart."

"He's really good for an Arab," Adina overheard a murmur a few seats away. *Arab?!* Adina felt her temperature rising, her forehead moistening, her lungs constricting.

"He'll condescend neither to lip nor cheek
In his garden blooms a rose not-yet-seen."

"Yes, other than his accent, his Hebrew is flawless," responded another voice.

The host shook Amir's hand as David yelled "Bravo!" and the rest of the audience applauded.

When Amir returned to his seat, Adina glued herself to the armrest and turned her back to him, ignoring his outstretched arm. She knew so little about him. It had never occurred to her that a man she would meet in Israel might not be Jewish. He certainly looked exotic—even next to the other Israelis— darker with coarser features. That's precisely why he had been so striking to her.

As the others made their way to the reception, Adina grabbed Amir by the arm and pulled him to the exit. She heard whispers of "Arab," "Hebrew poet," "Muslim," "sacred tongue," as they passed through the crowd.

As soon as they were out the door, Adina pushed him aside and ran home. She reached her front door perspiring and out of breath. Her vision was blurred by her tears, and she struggled to fit the key into the hole. Inside, she slammed the door and double-locked it behind her, in case he followed.

She collapsed on the sofa and picked up the dried Flower of Eden from the living room table. She held it in her hand, turning it over and over. Its softness and fragrance calmed her.

Why should his race and religious beliefs matter to her? He was first and foremost a human being, then a poet, then her lover, and only then a Muslim. Art was his religion, just as it was hers. That's what he lived for, lived by, just like her. They were alike in so many ways, got along so well, and their ethnicities had never before been an issue. She had played her most beautiful music under his influence. How could she continue playing without him?

Adina felt the flower crumble in her palm and threw its red and green remains like confetti on the floor. *He was, after all, an Arab, and Arabs were enemies of the Jews. How would her family react once they found out she was involved with an Arab? They would disown her. They would never invite her to another family celebration. She'd never see her parents and siblings again. He was forbidden to her.*

If they married, where would they live? In the Muslim Quarter of the Old City? In the Jewish Quarter? In West Jerusalem? In Ramallah? In the United States of America? Would they raise their children as Jews, or Muslims, or bohemians? The traditional prohibition against intermarriage was the one she'd always taken the most seriously and had never dated non-Jews back in America. How had she allowed herself to enter a relationship with a Muslim in Israel, of all places?

Adina fell asleep, fully clad in her cocktail dress and makeup, crying into the sofa pillow. She was woken early the next morning by a loud knock on her front door. "Adina, open up, it's me. We've got to talk." She recognized Amir's voice.

"Go away," she yelled, throwing her stiletto at the door. The noise it made upon impact startled even her.

"I thought you liked me."

Adina sat up, rose to her feet, smoothed her dress, wiped the black streaks around her eyes with a tissue and slowly advanced toward the door. She opened it but blocked the doorway with her body so he couldn't enter. They spoke, standing on either side of the door frame.

"I never lied to you; I never said I'm Jewish. I thought we had a special connection. What does it matter where my ancestors were born? Art knows no boundaries. Poetry is universal." It sounded rehearsed, but he had a point. Her love for him and her admiration for his poetry surpassed her repulsion. He pulled Adina into his arms. This time she did not resist and allowed him to embrace her.

When he left for work, she sat down to practice her violin. Adina did not feel the time go by, and only another knock at the door signaled that she had completed her two-hour rehearsal. "Just by the sound of your music I can tell you're feeling better," said Reut, a tall Israeli dancer with her hair plaited in a French braid. "Are you ready for our tour of the German Colony?"

Adina put her violin away in its case and together they ascended the stairs, past the windmill and through the park.

"I'm glad to see you smiling this morning. I was worried when you ran out of the hall right after the concert last night," said Reut, as the two women waited for the red traffic light to change so they could cross the street to Liberty Bell Park. "I wanted to congratulate you on your performance and Amir on his recitation."

"Really?" Adina met Reut's eyes for the first time.

"Yes, everyone was impressed. It's not often we encounter an Arab poet with such a mastery of the Hebrew language, sensitivity to its cadences, and insight into its connotations." Reut gracefully jumped over a pothole, as though it were part of a dance routine. "He's very talented."

"I thought so from the moment I met him," responded Adina, "but I didn't know he was Arab until last night."

"Isn't that Amir right there?" Reut pointed to the roof of a three-story house as they approached Emek Refaim Street. Amir was crouched, hoisting red tiles from a crane and placing them in neat rows on the roof. He waved when he saw Adina.

"Didn't you say he's an architect?" asked Reut.

"Yes, that's right," responded Adina, waving back to Amir, who almost lost his balance.

"What's he doing up there like a construction worker?" Reut inquired.

"I guess he's come to check that his plans are being carried out precisely and that the proper materials are used," suggested Adina, shrugging her shoulders.

"In any case, he's a great poet," asserted Reut. "After the reception, the colony's Board of Directors, on which I sit as the artists' representative, held its regular meeting. We decided by majority vote to grant Amir a fellowship and invite him to join our colloquia. We would like to publish some of his poetry in the monthly newsletter. Will you tell him the good news?"

"Of course!" Adina exclaimed. She wished she could tell him right away and began counting the minutes until she would see him again. She was so happy that she missed most of the mosaics, pointed arches, and ornate columns Reut pointed out during their walk. Adina told herself that she and Amir would come and celebrate at one of the German Colony's fancy restaurants, and then she would study the noteworthy features of the neighborhood.

After that, Amir became a regular at the artists' colloquia. Just as his presence at the colony's assemblies increased, so did his presence in Adina's home. His parents were apparently feeling better and the grant he had been awarded allowed him to hire a caretaker for them, so he was freer in the evenings. They started dining together, strolling together, and even spending the night together.

One day, they repotted Adina's geraniums. They had blossomed so profusely that they no longer fitted into the narrow container that had originally held them. Thanks to Amir's compost, the plant had regained its health and begun to sprout new branches. Together they unearthed several stalks and transferred them to a larger pot. They placed it on the stairs leading up to Adina's front door. So many flowers bloomed each day that many remained even after Adina had given a large split to Amir to plant in his own home.

They also became one another's muse and performed well in each other's company. He told her that her music inspired his poetry and she felt compelled to practice even harder. She composed music to accompany his poems, attempting to replicate the emotion of his verses in her own composition, which she felt ready to undertake for the first time. They were preparing to present the piece together at a gala event in honor of the colony's sponsor, a retired diamond trader who was flying in especially from Belgium.

—

Adina and Amir ascended the platform together, hand in hand. She sat down and positioned her violin as Amir picked up the microphone. "I would like to dedicate this poem, 'On the Qualities of Beauty,' to Adina." She covered her flushed cheeks with the palms of her hands and smiled at Amir. She then took a deep breath and played the introductory notes.

"A tulip cheek framed by raven ringlets
A rosebud surrounded by hyacinths," he began.

He paused for Adina's solo, then went on: *"How many enlightened souls for that face,"* he coughed, trying to cover up his mistake. Adina hadn't heard that instead of "face" (*panim*), he had said "sons" (*banim*), and proceeded with the piece.

Although Amir missed several beats, he resumed where he had left off: *"Shout out invocations of divine grace."*

Distracted by their lack of synchronization, Adina played the notes one octave too high, further confusing Amir who said *Allah* in place of *Elohi* ("divine"). His face blanched. The loud vibration of the strings produced by Adina's abrupt pause prevented the murmur that spread through the audience from reaching her ears.

As they descended the platform, the wealthy patron caught Adina's arm with the ivory handle of his walking stick, delaying her while Amir returned to their seats.

"Who is that man?" he asked in a loud whisper.

"My fiancé, Amir. A wonderful poet, isn't he?" she replied with a smile. She was surprised to hear herself saying "fiancé."

"Are you aware that he is Arab?"

"Yes, and I love him anyway."

"I refuse to continue supporting this colony if it accepts an Arab poet as a member. How dare he defile the sacred tongue?" He released Adina. She returned to her seat with her head held high.

—

Although he wasn't given a chance to read, Amir accompanied Adina to the next colloquium. Professor Rabinowitz of Yale University spoke of the role of poetry in mystical circles:

"In all mystical traditions we find a conflation of God, with whom the mystic ultimately wishes to unite, with the concept of beauty. The mystical journey is likened to the act of love. This is a recurrent motif in the writings and poetry of these sects. It starts with Plato's *Theory of the Forms*, especially as reinterpreted by the Neo-Platonists during the Renaissance, it appears in the *Song of Songs*, whose imagery was adopted by the Kabbalists, as well as in Saint Teresa of Avila's *Autobiography*. But the text that perhaps best exemplifies this theme is the allegorical Turkish Sufi poem, *Beauty and Love*, composed in the eighteenth century by Şeyh Galip. Consider this passage, for example, number five on your source sheet in English translation. This chapter is titled 'On the Qualities of Beauty.'

A tulip cheek framed by raven ringlets
A rosebud surrounded by hyacinths ...

How many enlightened souls for that face
Shout out invocations of divine grace

All delicacy, subtlety, all of a piece
Sweet gentleness, loveliness, without cease.

Notice how characteristics usually associated with God are ascribed to beauty, most explicitly 'divine grace,' 'gentleness,' and 'loveliness'. Beauty is described just as the poet envisions God."

After the lecture, a man and a woman in animated discussion approached the drinks table in the reception hall, just as Adina was pouring red wine for herself.

"What a fascinating lecture," exclaimed Reut.

"Yes … but that Sufi poem sounded very familiar," responded David.

"It reminded me of the poem Amir recited last time," she agreed.

Adina placed the wine bottle on the table, afraid to spill its contents with her shaking hands. "You're just saying that because he's Arab."

Reut turned to face Adina. "You know I'm the one who fought for his integration into the colony in the first place, despite the fact that he's Arab. But plagiarism is another matter altogether. Here, let's compare." She opened her purse and pulled out the newsletter, featuring the pieces presented the previous month. She turned to page three, where Amir's poem was printed in Hebrew letters.

"The same, word for word," she said, juxtaposing Amir's poem with the English source sheet from the lecture.

"I don't believe it," said Adina.

"Don't be stupid," retorted David. "You can tell just by looking at the format. It's identical: rhyming couplets." He tapped the ink with his forefinger.

Adina took the booklets from Reut's hand and examined the two poems. "But … Amir … I thought he wrote that poem … especially for me." She tossed the papers onto the edge of the table.

"It's not so hard to memorize a poem in translation," stated the man.

"He thought we'd never encounter Sufi literature," said Reut, wrapping her arm around Adina's heaving shoulders.

"Although, some cultures value the memorization and recitation of poetry over original composition," said David.

Adina grabbed the wine glass and marched to the corner of the hall, where she had left Amir chewing celery sticks dipped in hummus. She did not allow her eyes to meet his, nor did she return his smile. She tilted the goblet and spilled the purple liquid on his white shirt. He stood there, paralyzed, as she ran out the door.

—

Adina would have liked to sleep through the next day, but she once again got out of bed at dawn, after a sleepless night. She sat on the stool by the open window and placed the violin on her left shoulder, but could not produce a single note, nor move her bow with her numb fingers.

The entire week went by without music. Adina could not fall asleep at night. At sunrise she'd open the window and sit there until dusk, looking out, hoping to catch a glimpse of him.

On Saturday morning she sat by her window again, her eyes moving back and forth from the clouds to the geraniums.

"*Baba, Baba, ahkamna ala Ajmal wa Hub*," a young voice demanded under her window. She looked down and saw Amir, followed by five children and a woman with a brown headscarf tied under her double chin, carrying a picnic basket.

Amir picked up the smallest boy, pulled a paperback book out of his pocket, found the bookmark, and flipped to that page. She could sense from his tone and the cadence of the Arabic words that he recited the following verses:

"By cruel decree of unfavorable fate
Beauty fell in love with Love's shining face."

His voice became less and less audible as he climbed the stairs.

Adina rose from the stool, took one last look at the blossoming flowers, closed the shutters and then the windows, and left the stone house, carrying a suitcase in one hand and her violin in the other.

Dancing in Splendor

Laura was shaken from her slumber by the wailing siren that went off just as the bus exited Highway 6 toward Ben-Gurion International Airport. The bus rattled to a stop and the passengers clambered onto the hard shoulder, lying face down on the asphalt and covering their heads with their hands. *What are we doing so close to the gas tank?* she thought. *If it were to suffer a direct hit, we would all be consumed by flames.* But there was no time to run any farther. Her heart beat uncontrollably; all she could do was take long, deep breaths, just as Talya, their choreographer, had taught them the very first time a siren had gone off during rehearsals that summer.

The siren grew louder and louder for a full minute, its intonation rising and falling until it stopped abruptly, before an explosion, not unlike that which accompanies fireworks, was heard overhead, followed by the sound of combat planes setting off on their mission. Laura knew she should keep her head covered to protect herself from the falling debris but couldn't help raising her eyes and admiring the smoky white trail against the pitch-black sky, like a shooting star. Laura let out a sigh of relief, her breath rustling the reedy grass; Iron Dome had once again intercepted an incoming missile from Gaza. But it wasn't always as successful. Only the other day a rocket exploded in the courtyard outside her dorm, shattering her bedroom window.

Still lying on the ground, Laura thought of all the students who had gone home when the first siren sounded weeks earlier, rejoining their families in the central and northern parts of the country. Only she and a handful of other students remained on campus, the majority volunteering at the nearby hospital and seniors' residence. Laura had no choice as she had to attend rehearsals to prepare for their upcoming performance in Scotland. Besides, she had no other home to go to—her parents still resided in Canada, where she had lived until she graduated high school, at which point she decided to move to Israel, settling in Beer-Sheva. As Montreal's twin city, Beer-Sheva was a natural choice for a determined young woman who wished to make the desert bloom. She joined the university dance troupe immediately after enrolling in a degree program in environmental engineering—one of only three women on the course. It was there that she met Idan, a tall Israeli man with blue eyes and black hair, whose status had recently risen from boyfriend to fiancé.

Despite the heat and humidity of the mid-summer night, Laura's body shook and she could feel her agile muscles tensing. She heard rustling all around her as her friends started to rise. She swept the dry leaves, thorns, and earth from her black t-shirt and leggings, and climbed back onto the bus. All the excitement Laura had felt as they drove out of Beer-Sheva now dissipated at the realization that the rockets and sirens would follow them even to the very heart of the country. She was, now more than ever, looking forward to a week of tranquility and pleasure leading up to the troupe's first international performance, at the Edinburgh Fringe Festival, the world's largest arts festival.

As none of her friends could sleep any longer, the bus filled with enthusiastic chatter. Laura was glad to be in the company of her fellow dancers, with whom she had spent the greater part of the past month, rehearsing in the makeshift studio relocated to the underground bomb shelter on campus—all twenty of them crammed into a space much smaller than the Scottish stage, requiring spatial adjustments for the choreography.

Once at the airport, they learned that their flight was delayed, with a whole backlog of planes that had been unable to take off while missiles were targeting the airport.

—

As their plane finally landed in Scotland, the dancers looked out the window, admiring the green slopes and ancient stone castles; there was very little greenery in the Negev desert at this time of year, and the Old City of Beer-Sheva dated only as far back as the Ottoman Empire.

Walking down the cobblestone alleyways among the masses of people who had arrived in Edinburgh for the occasion, the dancers reveled in the colorful posters advertising the acts scheduled to take place that week: theater, spoken word, puppet shows, juggling, acrobatics, music, cabaret, and more. They were thrilled to spot the poster for their own dance performance, featuring an action shot of the entire troupe on tiptoe, brightly colored gowns swirling around their ankles. But they were soon distraught when, upon taking a closer look, they noticed that it had been defaced with a swastika.

The atmosphere around them was festive, resonating with thousands of vivid voices and the high-pitched wail of bagpipes. Though Laura forced herself to relax and enjoy the sights, her shoulders tensed every time church bells rang or bagpipes sounded in the vicinity.

Some of the performers had already taken their place on the open-air stages and were enchanting their audiences. Laura joined the crowd congregated around a puppeteer, who turned out to be a ventriloquist, manipulating puppets dressed in a traditional kilt.

As she ventured further down the lane, Laura glimpsed a dense crowd holding placards over their heads. Marching down the road toward her, the throng wore menacing facial expressions and their chanting was punctuated by drumbeats. Laura was once again startled to see the blue Star of David, her homeland's emblem, featured on each of the signs carried by the protesters, with a black swastika scrawled over it.

Laura ducked into a side street and watched in awe as the seemingly endless demonstration passed her by. The protesters' faces were painted with red, green, and black stripes, and checkered *keffiyeh* scarves were wrapped around their necks. They marched down the street screaming "evil dancers" at the top of their lungs.

"Evil dancers?" Laura's heart raced as she realized, horrified, that nearly ten thousand people had gathered to demonstrate against her troupe's performance at the festival. But what did dance have to do with the war? They had come here to escape from the rockets and sirens in pursuit of freedom of artistic expression, just like so many of the festival's participants; to show the world that culture may flourish even in a war zone. But these people were clearly uninterested in the beauty of art.

Laura felt her entire body quivering. She was more terrified here in Scotland than she had been in all the weeks of rocket attacks on Israel. At least in Beer-Sheva she knew the location of every bomb shelter and trusted the Iron Dome. Who would protect her against these people? She was fully exposed to their rage—directed precisely against her, though she held no responsibility for the war and was not involved in military action in any way. She had only come here to dance.

Laura ran down the street as fast as her long, muscular legs would carry her until she bumped into two other dancers from the troupe. "What's happened? You are positively pale!" they exclaimed, enfolding her in their arms.

Breathless, she told them about the demonstration she had just witnessed. Though they had not seen it, captivated as they were by a group of dancers accompanied by fiddlers, they'd heard distant drumbeats, thinking them to be the cheers of an appreciative crowd.

As they were due at rehearsal in one hour, the girls gathered up as many of the troupe's dancers as they could find before heading back to their hotel.

—

At exactly six o'clock, they lined up in their usual formation and began to warm up, stretching their arms, rotating their hips, and rolling their ankles. Since the choreographer had not yet shown up, Laura took the lead, turned on the music, and started performing her part. Several of the dancers joined her, but the majority leaned against the walls of the studio in ungraceful poses, chatting amongst themselves.

Laura was worried about Talya. It was so unlike her to be late to rehearsal—and after what she had witnessed that afternoon, she did not think it was safe for the young dancers to be roaming the streets of Edinburgh on their own. That was the real reason she had put on the music—a unique arrangement of medieval Judeo-Spanish liturgy—and started moving her limbs to its mesmerizing rhythm. The melody always exhilarated her, taking her mind off her mundane worries as the movement, leaping into the air and pirouetting at great heights, transported her to higher realms.

Only at 6:27 did the choreographer finally run into the studio, disheveled and out of breath. "Gather around me, girls, I've got bad news." The dancers disengaged from the walls and shuffled toward the center of the room, their satin costumes rustling as they glided over the parquet floor.

"As you may have heard, ten thousand people protested our participation in the festival today. There have been some pretty serious threats. The news has reached the authorities in Israel and they've decided to cancel our participation in the festival, afraid we may suffer the same fate as the Israeli athletes at the Munich Olympics. I've been on the phone with them for over an hour trying to persuade them, but no luck. Rehearsal is dismissed for tonight."

The dancers sighed in disbelief, their voices rising in unison— but Talya put up her hand, indicating that there was no point in arguing. Disappointed, Laura slipped her shoes back on, her dream shattered. She had anticipated this performance for months, but it was not to be. They'd come so close, but it remained elusive, and all for reasons of unfounded hatred.

—

Accompanied by several of her colleagues, Laura made her way to a rustic tavern near the hotel, the somber streets suddenly menacing and uninviting. The dancers settled themselves on high stools by the bar, slumped over despite their usual poise. Laura craved something truly strong and local, something homebrewed that she could not get elsewhere.

Though the pub was quite dim, she spotted a young woman sitting on her own a few stools down, perusing the festival program while sipping a golden liquid garnished with a cinnamon stick.

"Doesn't that look interesting?" she whispered to Noa.

"Yes, I wonder what it is."

Laura dislodged herself from her stool and took a few steps toward the woman. "Excuse me, what are you drinking?" she inquired.

The woman raised her head from the brochure. Laura noticed that she was leafing through the dance section, with several pages dog-eared already. "It's Glayva. I highly recommend it!"

"Thanks," exclaimed Laura. "Is that a Canadian accent I hear?"

"Yes, that's right," the woman confirmed.

"Awesome! What's your name? I'm Laura and I grew up in Montreal."

"It's nice to meet you, Laura. I'm Renée and I live in Toronto. Where do you live now?"

"I live in ..." she hesitated, "Israel."

Renée's eyes brightened. "I used to live in Bethlehem, right outside Jerusalem, until our Muslim neighbors started persecuting us because of our Christian faith. That's when my family moved to Toronto as refugees. We've been there ever since." Just the other day a rocket launched from Gaza landed in Bethlehem and Renée's former neighbors, a kindly elderly couple quite advanced in years, had been severely injured.

"What are you doing here?" Laura inquired.

"I love dance and have always wanted to attend the festival and watch some of the world's luminaries in action, but it was particularly important to me this year as I'm opening a dance studio in Toronto next spring and wanted to get some inspiration, some exposure to the most avant-garde styles and techniques."

"That's wonderful!" Laura exclaimed. "We were supposed to perform on Thursday, during the closing act," she swept her hand in the direction of her fellow troupe members, "but, sadly, we just found out that our performance has been cancelled for political reasons."

"You mustn't give in to their threats," insisted Renée. "It's your slot; you've come all the way here and you've got such beautiful things to show the world, I am sure."

Laura nodded her head, but her eyes remained downcast.

All of a sudden, her face lit up. "We're both Canadian," she exclaimed. "Why don't we ask to fill that slot as two Canadian dancers sharing our individual stories from the Middle East? There's no way they would object to such a collaboration."

A smile slowly spread across Renée's face. "I guess this drink really is strong. It must have gotten to my head. I would never agree to it under any other circumstance; I came here as an observer, not as a dancer, but I believe this is for a good cause." Laura and Renée clinked their glasses and agreed to meet again the following morning.

—

Talya wouldn't hear of it—the protesters had made it clear that the lives of the Israeli dancers were in danger, and she felt personally responsible for their safety. Laura insisted that she would appear as a Canadian living in Israel. She wasn't afraid;

she had a valuable message to relay and would not be intimidated or cast aside. Talya promised to bring Laura's proposal before the organizers.

Laura and Renée spent the next three days in fervent rehearsal, pausing only to attend those performances they absolutely could not miss. It took them some time to formulate a concept that would capture their two distinct experiences of the Middle East and seamlessly blend the choreographic styles they had come to embody. After many hours of deliberation and trial and error, they consolidated a program they both felt comfortable with: they would enter and exit the stage together, but would each have a solo in the middle.

Laura asked her friend Noa to lend her costume to Renée, since they shared a similar physique and she no longer needed it. Renée adamantly refused to wear red, the color of blood and passion; so they soaked the satin in blue dye, imparting it with a deep indigo tinge that complemented Renée's blue eyes.

—

They were finally ready for their impromptu performance. An erratum sheet had been printed and distributed to all of the festival's attendees, framing Laura and Renée as "two Canadian dancers of Middle Eastern origin, who will be sharing their unique perspectives on the devastating situation currently rending the hearts of Palestinians and Israelis."

Laura's troupe filled the first two rows of the auditorium, cheering for Laura with all the enthusiasm they could muster, though they sat trembling in their seats, afraid that an itinerant hothead would enter the auditorium and start shooting. Though they had tried to enjoy the past few days, and attended many shows with all the free time they had after rehearsals were cancelled, they were flustered. Each had done her part to help Laura's initiative come to fruition—designing a new poster, distributing flyers, making a new soundtrack, adjusting her dress, doing her hair and makeup, and offering feedback on the choreography—and they sincerely hoped the show would proceed without interruption.

Backstage, Laura was unaware that she was pulling strands of hair out of her tightly braided bun, butterflies fluttering in the depths of her knotted intestines. She hadn't heard from her fiancé, Idan, in three days, ever since he had been called up by the army for reserve duty. She knew that his battalion was due to enter Gaza to dismantle weapon-smuggling tunnels and confiscate illegal ammunition. Though it was only natural that he would not be allowed to use his cell phone while in action, Laura could not help but worry. News of more and more soldiers—many of them about to be married—killed in Gaza, was announced every single day, and she could not bear the anxiety.

Just the week before, she and her boyfriend had driven into the desert to the big crater at Mitzpe Ramon, where they thought the rockets would not reach them, and stayed up all night watching the meteor shower. The stillness and peacefulness of the dark, star-lit desert sky was a welcome respite after the month of shootings and explosions they had just experienced. It was there, in their cozy tent under the shooting stars, that Idan had proposed and become her fiancé.

What if he, too, like so many others, never came out of Gaza? Their love had just started to blossom and they deserved a chance to make it flourish. They had made such exciting plans to travel the world together and raise bilingual kids, and the members of the company had even promised to perform a special dance at the wedding. On the plane over, Laura had sketched her dream wedding dress. Would she ever have a chance to wear it or would it, instead, serve as his shroud?

Shaking from head to toe, Laura stepped onto the stage. She did not know how she would maintain her balance, her knees threatening to buckle under. But as soon as the first notes sounded, Laura was suffused with their magic and transported to exotic lands, dancing in all her glory alongside Renée, as though performing before a sultan in a majestic palace.

Just as she and Renée took their bows, honored with a standing ovation, fireworks were shot up into the sky, marking the culmination of the weeklong festival. At that moment, Laura's poise abandoned her, and she let out a shriek, grabbed Renée by the wrist, and pulled her into the safety of the wings.

Rose among the Thorns

My grandmother, Nona Paloma, has been enamored with *El Cantar de los Cantares* for as long as I can remember. As a young child, I too became enthralled by its mysteriousness and enchantment.

I remember those eerie nights when my siblings and I slept at my grandparents' house in Ein Kerem, a serene village on the slopes of Jerusalem's hills, with stone houses and lofty pine trees. My grandmother would put us to bed in the upstairs bedroom with the vaulted ceiling and painted floor tiles singing:

"I am asleep but my heart is awake, the voice of my beloved knocks. 'Open up, my sister, my beloved, my dove, my innocent one; for dew suffuses my head, drops of the night fill my locks.'"

On those nights I would have the strangest dreams. My eyelids would grow heavy as I counted the stars, brighter than anything I ever saw in the city, and smelled the fragrance of almond blossoms, penetrating the chamber through the open window. At that moment a procession of strangers would appear to me, claiming to be my ancestors. Though they all bore some resemblance to my grandmother, I did not recognize them.

One woman had my grandmother's dimpled cheek and deep-set brown eyes, and wore a gold crown on her head. Another was young and freckled and sat at a small Damascene table hunched over a sewing machine, her feet rhythmically tapping the pedal as though it were a piano, as her hands gracefully slid the voluminous velvet across the wooden table inlaid with mother-of-pearl. Yet another, wearing a satin gown, sat in a rose garden strumming the lute. The water flowing from the fountain behind her punctuated my grandmother's humming as she rocked in her chair, waiting for us to fall asleep.

Like the women in my dreams, Nona Paloma wore a gold chain around her neck, with a pomegranate-shaped pendant suspended from it. Its scarlet jewels—garnets, my birthstone—emitted an unusual radiance. Curled up in my grandmother's lap, I couldn't resist handling it, my fingers drawn to its cool, smooth surface.

Turning the pendant over in the palm of my hand, I would ask, "What does it say here?"

She would recite the engraved verses from the *Song of Songs*:

"My beloved is a locked garden, a sealed fountain;
A pomegranate orchard with exquisite fruits."

The necklace never left my grandmother's neck. She never let me try it on, no matter how much I implored.

"This necklace has been in the family for a thousand years; one day it will be yours," she promised, tracing the contours of my face with her soft fingers.

—

Nona Paloma refused to serve dinner on Friday nights, when the entire family gathered at her home to celebrate the Sabbath, until my grandfather, Nono Salomon, finished chanting all eight chapters of *El Cantar de los Cantares* to her. Enthroned in his chair at the head of the table, like his namesake, his melodious voice serenaded her at the end of every week:

"Ec tú hermosa, mi companyera;
Ec tú hermosa;
tus ojos como de palombino."

You are beautiful, my beloved;
You are beautiful;
Your eyes are doves.

The flickering flames atop the tall silver candlesticks accentuated Nona Paloma's high cheekbones. Caressing her hand, Nono Salomon would gaze into her brown eyes with a tenderness that always moved me to tears.

Exasperated by the length of the ceremony, Tía Sarah would interrupt my grandfather's recitation:

"The children are getting hungry!"

"*Bavajadas*, they are no longer babies," was my grandmother's usual response. Winking at my grandfather, she'd continue, "Let them be nourished by their grandparents' love, a love upon which the world's very existence depends." I always found my grandparents' connection inspiring and hoped that one day I, too, would love and be loved by a faithful partner.

Setting the leather-bound tome on the white tablecloth embroidered with silver thread, my grandfather would rise to his feet and kiss my grandmother's outstretched hand. Her dimple would become apparent as she returned his smile. All those gathered around the table would then join in greeting the guardian angels and sanctifying the Sabbath with the blessing over the wine. I could almost see the angels, donning translucent gowns of white light, their iridescent wings fluttering as they hovered around the table.

Only then would the steaming delicacies be brought to the table—lamb tagine with dried fruits, walnuts, and caramelized onions seasoned with cinnamon, cardamom, and cloves, rice with slivered almonds and raisins, and a green salad dressed with pomegranate vinaigrette, freshly extracted from the fruit of the tree in the garden. These were the dishes I craved whenever I visited my grandparents. The food was as delectable to the palate as to the eye, its aromas filling the dining room.

—

When my grandparents approached their golden anniversary, I sought an appropriate gift to mark the occasion. I wandered into the Old City through Zion Gate and walked the narrow cobblestone alleys to the Cardo, the Roman marketplace at the heart of the Jewish Quarter, lined with ornate classical columns.

I knew I would recognize the ideal gift when I saw it.

I soon stumbled on a small gallery—wedged between a jeweler's studio and a ceramic cooperative—with bold abstract paintings flanking the arched doorway.

Bells chimed as I entered the vaulted chamber. My eyes jumped from canvas to canvas of vividly colored birds in flight, until I was drawn to a lone painting on the opposite wall of the gallery that differed from all the others in its small scale and subdued tonality. Framed in silver, it depicted a pomegranate tree with luscious red fruits and a pair of white doves nestled in its branches.

"This is it," I muttered.

I knew how my grandmother adored the pomegranate tree in her garden, wrapping each individual fruit blossom to protect it from insects, and how much she prized her necklace. I couldn't help but think of the pair of doves on the paper as my grandparents, eternally faithful in their love for one another.

A woman of slight stature waltzed across the floor. Her long blond hair illumined her face, and she lit up the dim space with every step.

"Isn't it beautiful?" she asked. "It's one of my favorites."

"Yes, it's magnificent," I responded. "I'm looking for a gift for my grandparents' fiftieth anniversary. They will love its elegant simplicity."

"I'm sure they will," affirmed the gallery owner.

"My grandfather's name is Salomon and my grandmother is Paloma—a dove. It's as though this painting was made specially for them."

"I had a feeling about it when I painted it. I always like to have an idea of the person for whom the artwork is intended and knew the doves would have special significance. Do you know that the painting contains the entire *Song of Songs*?"

My heart skipped a beat. I hadn't noticed. I took a step forward and observed the work up close. I could now see the jagged lines delineating the leaves, birds, and branches consisted of minuscule Hebrew script in colored ink, meticulous work that must have taken days of concentration to complete.

I read the words making up the red fruits topped with coronets:

Let us rise and head to the vineyards to see if the vine has budded, if the vine-blossom has opened, if the pomegranates have flowered; there I will give you my love.

A shiver ran down my spine. There could not be a more perfect gift.

The woman extended her hand. "I am Bina Ravel, by the way. What's your name?"

I hesitated, but somehow knew I could trust her.

"My name is Kitra Vardi." An electrifying energy emanated from her fingertips as we shook hands.

"Kitra Vardi is a wonderful name for a poet," she exclaimed. "Why don't you come back here tomorrow evening? I will be hosting a gathering of artists and writers and would like to introduce you to them. I will have the painting all wrapped up and ready for you to take home to your grandparents then."

With that, she pirouetted across the room to another customer, her sequined bell sleeves swirling around her arms like outspread wings. I did not know how she had intuited my most profound desire to become a poet, but it was then I started taking my ambition seriously and cherishing the uniqueness of my name Kitra, a name that had until then been a source of tremendous grief and countless taunts by classmates mocking its Aramaic origin. I soon became a regular visitor to Bina's gallery, taking her scattered verses and polished poems to read.

My grandmother's hands shook as she unwrapped the parcel. "It's a very thoughtful gift," she said. "Of all my grandchildren, you've always been my kindred spirit."

—

The painting was displayed on a prominent wall in the living room and I admired it every time I visited. When I turned twenty-five and was still not married, my twin sisters, Tiferet and Ateret, convinced me I needed to take urgent action as I might be running out of time. Nona Paloma assured me that my intended was on his way. "You've got such exotic beauty, *hermosa* Kitra, I have no doubt you will soon meet a deserving young man." She urged me to try the method she had used to conjure my grandfather more than half a century before. "Read *El Cantar de los Cantares* in its entirety for the next forty days. It's a sacred tradition in our family. Just don't tell your mother I told you to do this. She'll say I'm brainwashing you with my primitive superstitions, even though she herself used this very same method to meet your father."

Though I considered it highly improbable that my mother would have engaged in such practices in her youth and was unsure if I believed in the power of the incantation, I thought it wouldn't hurt to try. "Don't worry about it, Nona. It will be our secret." I sealed the pact with a kiss on her lined cheek.

I spent the next forty nights reading the *Song of Songs* from beginning to end before turning off the lights in my bedroom. Perched on my narrow bed, I savored the sound of every syllable I enunciated. I tried to imagine what my beloved would look like and how we would sit around the dinner table on Friday nights reciting these same verses to each other.

I am the lily of Sharon, the rose of the valleys.
Like a rose among the thorns, so is my beloved among the maidens.

Perhaps I was the rose among the thorns, "*la rosa entre los espinos,*" as Nona Paloma sometimes called me, unable to truly open my heart to another; perhaps I had put up a prickly façade, internalizing the rose's properties bequeathed by my surname Vardi, meaning "roselike."

I always waited until my parents had gone to bed before beginning the recitation, but instead of conjuring my beloved, the procession of ancestors reappeared in my dreams. I usually forgot about them by the time I woke up in the morning, but continued to feel unsettled for the rest of the day.

—

When nearly a year had passed and I still wasn't engaged, I decided to take more drastic measures. Reading the *Song of Songs* had proved insufficient; it would behoove me to transcribe the text in order to contemplate every letter. I made my way to the Old City, where my feet instinctively led me to Bina's gallery, and asked her to teach me how to create my own micrography, like the one she had sold me several years before as a gift for my grandparents.

"The technique is really quite simple; you just have to be in the right state of mind."

"What do you mean?"

"Start by envisioning an image from the *Song of Songs*."

"How about '*the rose among the thorns*'?"

"That will do. Begin by outlining the rose in pencil and decide where you would like the biblical text to begin and end. Use colored pens to inscribe the verses along the outline. Once the ink is dry you can erase the pencil marks, et voilà!"

I made several sketches, my handwriting becoming more compact with each attempt, but I felt that it was all mere craft and artifice.

Bina examined my drawings. "They lack soul. I want you to do this on the next full moon. Meditate on the following verses from the *Zohar*, the *Book of Radiance*, and its mystical interpretation of the *Song of Songs*:

A song that is holy of holies
As the highest divine name is crowned by it
Because all of its words are love and joy."

"I thought you weren't supposed to study the *Zohar* before the age of forty. Isn't it dangerous?"

"Not if it's done with the proper intention," Bina reassured me. "Besides, the best things in life come with a risk." I was willing to risk it for the prospect of marriage.

Sitting at my desk, I closed my eyes and contemplated the verses Bina had dictated. The brilliance of the full moon penetrated my eyelids. Each ray of moonlight dissolved into the seven colors of the spectrum as it traversed the prism of my retina.

I opened my eyes and the white page glowed in the luminescence of the moonlight, forming a halo around the rose petals I had unknowingly traced with my eyes closed. I felt my own words flowing out of my heart, mingling with the sacred scriptures, as the ink flowed from the pen. I had never shown my poetry to anyone except Bina. She was the first person who ever believed in me, the only one who encouraged me to pursue my passion.

I sought to conceal my poetic words in minuscule script illegible to the naked eye, ashamed of the desperation and vulnerability they articulated:

Thou shall not take God's name in vain
Why did you betray me?
Why did you breathe the four letters of the holiest name
LOVE אהבה
Crowning the common name?

You did not allow the Shekhinah שכינה to dwell among us
And your soul did not cling to mine with the kiss of your mouth
For you are a wall, a locked garden

You have sought only to nestle your head
In my fragrant chest
To caress my dark skin

But my heart is awake and your heart is deaf to the throbbing
between my breasts.

This was my first poem to take concrete form, the words
shaping the rose's red petals, green leaves, and brown thorns.
As I placed the Hebrew letters side by side on the paper, I
felt a burning sensation in my fingertips and an unexpected
warmth in my heart.

Readers' Guide

The idea for this collection started taking shape after I joined a walking tour of Jerusalem following in the footsteps of poetesses, and visited the historical homes of Rachel Bluwstein-Sela, Zelda Schneurson-Mishkovsky, Leah Goldberg, and Else Lasker-Schüler, all the while reciting their extraordinary verses and seeing with my own eyes some of the cityscapes that had inspired their poetry.

Ticho House gained personal significance for me as a site of cultural activity in Jerusalem when I started working as an editor at The Israel Museum. I contributed to exhibitions held at Ticho House, now a branch of the Museum, and was so moved by its charm that I chose it as the venue for my wedding in July 2013. Ticho House has continued to inspire Jerusalem's contemporary writers and artists, such as the jazz musicians who regularly perform there as part of the popular wine and jazz nights, or the late Aharon Appelfeld, who I would often see sitting at a corner table in the café, writing a chapter a day of his newest novel, longhand.

Throughout this collection of literary and historical fiction, the characters struggle with their fragmented and often clashing identities as women, spouses, Jews, and migrant artists, in an attempt to reconcile their artistic practice and commitment to European aesthetics with their ethical world-view and devotion to the values of the fledgling State. At times they also suffer persecution because of their gender and ethnicity. Yet they remain committed to the pursuit of their art as a fulfillment of their social responsibility and true passion.

The narratives in this collection explore universal themes of identity, belonging, assimilation, and displacement while touching on aspects of the Arab-Israeli conflict, tensions between Israel and the Diaspora, and the complexity of human relationships. This collection of linked short stories captures a vivid image of Jerusalem, past and present, through the eyes of its diverse inhabitants. As such, it gives a voice to the women writers, artists, and poets of Israel's founding generation, imagining what their perspective might have been at that foundational stage in the country's political, social, and cultural development. Though they were not always appreciated, their love for the city of Jerusalem never wavered, and they continued to maintain their passion for their art.

1. What are the challenges faced by these characters as women?
2. What are the challenges faced by these characters as migrants?
3. What are the challenges faced by these characters as artists?
4. How does childlessness affect these women's artistic processes and output?
5. How does the European aesthetic legacy infuse these artists' practices in the nascent State of Israel? Could there be such a thing as a purely Israeli style, independent of external influences?

6. Can a nation's literature be created in a vacuum or are literary models always necessary, even if drawn from other cultures?

7. These stories present the poetic works of these women in English translation. What is the value of translation? What is the significance of the demand for original Hebrew writing in the context of early Israeli statehood? Do you agree that a poet can only write in their mother tongue or can a writer express themselves in any language they choose?

8. Discuss the tension between the arts and the sciences in these stories.

9. Several of the poets in these stories were also interested in drawing and painting. What is the connection between literature and the visual arts? Do you think an artist needs to specialize in a particular discipline or can they experiment with different art forms?

10. Some of the characters were engaged in other professions alongside their artistic pursuits. Do you think artists should devote themselves entirely to their art or can it be enriched by other vocations?

Representations of Jerusalem in the Poetry and Paintings of Else Lasker-Schüler

In November 1932, Expressionist poet and painter Else Lasker-Schüler (1869–1945) was awarded the Kleist Prize, Germany's most prestigious literary distinction for lifetime achievement. She gained recognition as an important literary and cultural figure in Germany and as a significant contributor to the modern German art scene. Ironically, only months later, as a result of Hitler's rise to power in January 1933, Lasker-Schüler was labelled a degenerate Jewish artist and forced to witness the public burning of her books. She fled Germany and eventually settled in Jerusalem. Even though she always considered herself a German artist and an integral part of German culture, she was proud of her Jewish heritage, which became a primary source of inspiration for her.

The collection of poetry titled *Hebrew Ballads*, published in 1913 with some of her own illustrations, is considered one of the greatest literary-artistic achievements of her career. Her poetic language evokes the history that binds all Jewish people together as an everlasting nation. The poem that best conveys this idea is "Mein Volk" ("My People") of 1905:

The rock decays
From which I spring
To sing my songs of God …
[…]
When to the East, awesomely,
The decaying rock of bone,
My people,
Cries out to God.[1]

Throughout her *Hebrew Ballads*, Lasker-Schüler drew inspiration from biblical texts as well as mystical kabbalistic works, which had fascinated her since childhood. Lasker-Schüler's treatment of the Bible is unique due to her personal identification with its characters, particularly with Joseph. She adopted the pseudonym "Jussuf, Prince of Thebes" (the royal city of the ancient Egyptian empire). In her drawings and self-portraits, Prince Jussuf appears as a youth in profile, adorned with Middle Eastern jewels and garments, with a crescent moon and a Star of David imprinted on his cheek. Through her choice of artistic persona, "she rebelled against the conventions of the day, which assigned women the sort of passive, marginal role she refused to adopt. By means of Jussuf she could portray herself as she wished to be: an artist free of the shackles of cultural norms, and a universal figure who united the two sexes, the three monotheistic religions, and the past and the present."[2]

The appropriation of this persona set in an unspecified time and Eastern location was crucial to the transcendence of the artist's own, often unbearable, reality and to her pursuit of universal acceptance as a Jewish artist. Lasker-Schüler's "game of hide-and-seek behind the mask of the prince created a space for the chaotic creativity in her writing. In

Eastern costume, her serious artistic game guaranteed [...] exotic untouchability."[3] Lasker-Schüler's particular exoticism demonstrated her wish "to be appreciated as a unique Jewish artist and visionary who was developing a new type of art that bridged the cultural gap between East and West."[4]

One of the ways in which she achieved this goal was by using biblical stories as contexts for her meditations about her fragile emotional state, imbuing biblical figures with the same artistic interests and emotional complexities as herself, rather than conceiving of them as idealized heroes from the past. Lasker-Schüler coined the term *Wild Jews* to describe these biblical figures, whom she regarded as "exceptional human beings [...] characterized by passion, bravery, and the ability to produce great art."[5] The *Wild Jews* appear repeatedly in both her poetry and paintings and express her desire for the revival of Jewish culture based on ancient biblical roots. Her lithograph, *Der Bund der Wilden Juden* (*The Association of the Wild Jews*) of 1923 depicts several figures in Middle Eastern outfits and headdresses. A Star of David framed by a crescent moon, Prince Jussuf's symbol, appears on the central figure's cheek, conveying the artist's belief that the biblical figure of Joseph epitomizes the *Wild Jew* she admired so much. A Star of David shines above the group, guiding them in all their endeavors. Lasker-Schüler believed that the *Wild Jews* would "serve for both Jews and non-Jews as proud examples of the Jewish past and as role-models for the future."[6] Although she adopted Jewish texts primarily as an artistic device to soothe her internal emotional conflicts, Lasker-Schüler was also concerned with promoting the work of Jewish artists and thus increasing the respect of the local Jewish community in the eyes of the Germans. In her own words, "every child in Germany knows how I bestowed honour on our people there."[7]

Even though she was at the forefront of German culture and highly admired by contemporary artists, Lasker-Schüler never felt completely at home in Germany. She always yearned for the biblical Land of Israel, which she imagined as a utopian paradise. By setting much of her poetry and illustrations in the Middle East, Lasker-Schüler demonstrated her love for Israel and expressed her yearning for its re-establishment as the homeland of the Jewish People. In *Das Hebräerland* (*The Land of the Hebrews*), a book of poetry containing eight of her original illustrations published in 1937, she described her experiences in the Holy Land and glorified Jerusalem as "God's veiled bride [...] the observatory of the hereafter, the heaven before Heaven."[8] This passage resonates with descriptions of Jerusalem in all its splendor at the time of redemption in the classical Jewish sources, specifically the sixteenth-century liturgical poem *Lekha Dodi*, in which Jerusalem is referred to as God's bride, itself based on a verse from the book of *Isaiah* (62:5).

Despite the harsh conditions the artist experienced in Jerusalem, Lasker-Schüler claimed that "God adores Jerusalem and has enclosed it in his heart. He has chosen this eternal city of cities."[9] Lasker-Schüler intended her book to comfort Diaspora Jews, who were then suffering through the Holocaust, as suggested by her statement that Jerusalem "blesses those who long for its blessing, the devout city comforts those who wish to be comforted."[10] Lasker-Schüler herself was somewhat comforted by Jerusalem one Sabbath as she sat on her balcony and saw a group of eighty Jews walking toward the Western Wall along Jaffa Road. She was so overwhelmed by this sight that she wrote in *Das Hebräerland*, "this gobelin, woven of eternal threads, the veins and silken hairs of the ancient tribes of Judah, was tattooed over time into the very skin of my temples."[11]

For Lasker-Schüler, verbal and visual expression were so closely entwined that she often illustrated a poem with the same pen with which she wrote it. Her painting *On Jaffa Road* translates this poetic description into a visual image. It depicts Jews of different ethnicities on their way to the Western Wall, against the background of Jerusalem's stone buildings, dressed in brightly colored garments and headdresses. In the right foreground, a little boy is affectionately held by a man, presumably his father. As the boy is depicted hovering in the air, Jerusalem is imbued with a sense of mystical timelessness. Arabs riding a donkey pass the group of Jews, reflecting the artist's conviction that Jews and Arabs can co-exist peacefully. The image expresses the artist's vision of Jerusalem in messianic times, when peace will reign. The same message is communicated in *Rabbi Prado in Palestine*, which depicts Rabbi Prado in deep meditation in the middle of a group of admiring youths in oriental garb. He is dressed in an exotic version of traditional Jewish garments, including the *talit*, *tzizit*, and head covering, decorated with the Star of David. This same symbol also crowns the golden domed structure in the background. The artist thus expressed her yearning for the re-establishment of Jerusalem's majesty, transforming it once again into the focal point of Jewish spirituality.

Lasker-Schüler concluded that "the blessed land needed a poet to come extol it,"[12] identifying herself with other poets who praised Jerusalem through the generations. She modelled her artistic works directly on Hebrew poetry, to such an extent that she regarded her own poems as Hebrew texts. When the poet Avraham Kariv offered to translate her poetry into Hebrew, she protested, claiming that it was originally composed in Hebrew.

As in the *Song of Songs*, Lasker-Schüler expressed her love for Israel in a religio-erotic manner, as a way of simultaneously communicating her yearning for the land and for the people she loved. She admired the *Song of Songs* and it was a major source of inspiration, as demonstrated by her poem "Shulamite," named after its heroine:

O, from your sweet mouth
I learned too much of bliss!
[...]
And my soul burns away in the evening colors
Of Jerusalem.[13]

She interprets the *Song of Songs* as a prophecy of the restoration of Jerusalem, a wish that can only be realized once the poet's emotional desires are fulfilled.

This same poetic motif recurs in "Jerusalem," which appeared in her last poetry collection, *Mein Blaues Klavier* (*My Blue Piano*), of 1943:

God formed out of his spine: Palestine
Out of one single bone: Jerusalem.

[...] Our holy city turned to stone.

[...] Were you to come—
To this ancestral land—
You would reproach me like a little child:
Jerusalem, arise and live again![14]

Lasker-Schüler alternates between love of land and love of man and links passion for others with spiritual yearning, since she believed that the communion of human beings has the power to bring us closer to the Divine. In this poem, the fulfilment of emotional desires brings about the redemption of Jerusalem in three stages: first, the mythical creation of Jerusalem from God's bone, then the historical selection of Jerusalem as God's city, and finally the emotional re-awakening of Jerusalem in the poet's consciousness.[15] As Lasker-Schüler affirmed in *Das Hebräerland*, "through the poetry of my *Hebrew Ballads*, I have contributed to the building of Palestine; I have not been idle in God's work."[16]

The artist and the city of Jerusalem are connected in a symbiotic bond whereby Jerusalem awaits the fulfilment of the poet's emotional desire to regain its original glory, while the poet anticipates Jerusalem's transformation into an idealized city to work out her emotions. The appropriation of Jerusalem as her own intimate realm is revealed in Lasker-Schüler's drawings of Jerusalem, particularly in *Thebes with Jussuf* of 1923. This painting depicts crowded buildings with her self-portrait as Prince Jussuf looking out of a blue window. Just as in Jerusalem, there are buildings in the same neighborhood adorned with a Star of David and a crescent moon. Even though she named it Thebes, a Hebrew inscription reads "Shalem," Jerusalem's biblical name. This inscription may also be read as "Shalom," alluding to redeemed Jerusalem in which peace will prevail. These elements demonstrate the artist's yearning for Jerusalem's re-awakening, but also her appropriation of Jerusalem as her sole emotional possession, since Jussuf is the only inhabitant of the city. In other words, "Lasker-Schüler was not depicting a real place in this world, but rather her own Jerusalem, which adjoins the Garden of Eden and cannot be defined in terms of space and time."[17]

Despite her ability to transform Jerusalem into a paradise in her artworks, Lasker-Schüler was not oblivious to the imperfect reality of her life in the city. Most disappointing was the lack of appreciation she encountered there among her fellow Jews. Although she did have a small circle of admirers in the *Der Kraal* group, a literary club founded in Jerusalem in 1941, consisting mostly of German émigré writers and artists, who regularly attended her literary soirées, many people were unsympathetic to her refusal to learn the Hebrew language. Just as she had felt underestimated as a Jewish artist in Germany, she continued feeling uncomfortable as a German poet in Jerusalem. In her own words, "the same Jerusalem that I have glorified so in my poems offers me no home."[18]

This sentiment of homelessness is re-iterated in her last collection of poetry, *Mein Blaues Klavier* published in 1943, dedicated to her "friends in the cities of Germany—and to those who like myself were driven out, and are now scattered throughout the world."[19] The sense of not truly belonging anywhere finds its visual parallel in her self-portrait, *The Scared-off Poetess*, in which the unappreciated artist chooses to leave her home. Though Lasker-Schüler depicts herself as that same youthful figure in profile used throughout her life to portray Prince Jussuf, this painting expresses vulnerability and sorrow, demonstrated by the curved neck and hands holding on to another person for support. As indicated by the artist's scribbling on the painting, it was first drawn in hospital in 1933 while recovering from the Nazi attack that drove her out of Germany, and re-worked nine years later in 1942 to convey her negative experience in Jerusalem. It is significant that she conflates the lack of appreciation by her own people with the traumas inflicted by Nazi Germany, and that both events find expression in the same painting.

Lasker-Schüler's strength as an artist derived from her ability to turn her powerful emotions into artworks expressing a universal spiritual yearning. She used biblical sites, events, and characters as poetic frameworks for her emotional experiences and interpreted them to suit her artistic needs. Gottfried Benn, her lover and fellow poet, described Else Lasker-Schüler as the "greatest lyrical poet Germany ever had. The subject matter of her poems was mainly Jewish, her imagination essentially oriental, but her language was German."[20] Her adoption of Expressionist tenets allowed her to contend with her religious, social, and political concerns by allowing her passionate writing and drawing to emerge directly from her heart, without concern for limitations of time, space, and logic. As Gottfried Benn wrote to Lasker-Schüler when she was awarded the Kleist Prize, "the Kleist Prize, so often sullied [...] was once again ennobled by being awarded to you. Congratulations to German poetry!"[21] The Kleist Prize was the ultimate acknowledgement that Else Lasker-Schüler's art, with its overt Jewish content, had gained acceptance as a genuine component of modern German culture.

1 Audri Durchslag and Jeanette Litman-Demeestere, trans. and ed., *Else Lasker-Schüler's Hebrew Ballads and Other Poems* (Philadelphia: The Jewish Publication Society of America, 1980), 59.

2 Irit Salmon, ed., *I and I: Drawings by Else Lasker-Schüler, Based on the Exhibit at the Ticho House* (Jerusalem: The Israel Museum, 1997), 23–24.

3 Donna K. Heizer, *Jewish-German Identity in the Orientalist Literature of Else Lasker-Schüler, Friedrich Wolf, and Franz Werfel* (Columbia: Camden House, Inc., 1996), 40.

4 Ibid., 44.

5 Ibid., 37–38.

6 Ibid., 37–38.

7 Betty Falkenberg, *Else Lasker-Schüler: A Life* (London: McFarland & Company, Inc., 2003), 156.

8 Durchslag and Litman-Demeestere, *Else Lasker-Schüler's Hebrew Ballads*, 51.

9 Ibid., 51.

10 Ibid., 51.

11 Falkenberg, *Else Lasker-Schüler*, 153.

12 Durchslag and Litman-Demeestere, *Else Lasker-Schüler's Hebrew Ballads*, 53.

13 Ibid., 75.

14 Ibid., 81.

15 Avidov Lipsker, "Literary and Visual Expressions of Jerusalem in the Poetry and Painting of Else Lasker-Schüler," in *A Woman in Jerusalem*, edited by Tova Cohen and Joshua Schwartz (Ramat-Gan: Bar-Ilan University, Ingburg-Renart Center for Jerusalem Studies, 2002), 156–157.

16 Durchslag and Litman-Demeestere, *Else Lasker-Schüler's Hebrew Ballads*, xi.

17 Salmon, *I and I*, 29.

18 Durchslag and Litman-Demeestere, *Else Lasker-Schüler's Hebrew Ballads*, ix.

19 Falkenberg, *Else Lasker-Schüler*, 174.

20 Durchslag and Litman-Demeestere, *Else Lasker-Schüler's Hebrew Ballads*, ix.

21 Falkenberg, *Else Lasker-Schüler*, 146.

Acknowledgements

The spark for this collection originated with my Master's thesis for the Shaindy Rudoff Graduate Program in Creative Writing at Bar-Ilan University, under the supervision of Prof. Allen Hoffman. The seed has blossomed over nearly two decades into its present form, after Fred Casden suggested that I expand the initial two stories, "Late Blossoms" and "Degeneration," into a collection of linked stories set at the Ticho House salon.

Thank you to my dear friends, Shelley Adler and Mizmor Watzman, who were there with me at Ticho House when the initial idea came to me. Thank you as well to my first readers, Dr. Lucy Rose Fischer, Dr. Petre Santry, Dr. Emily McAvan, Fred Casden, Anav Silverman, and Dr. Jahanzeb Khan. I appreciate your insights and encouragement. Many thanks to the writers who have endorsed this book, as well as to Rhonda Douglas of Resilient Writers for the generous scholarship to her First Book Finish Program, during which I completed this manuscript.

I am grateful to the amazing historical women who inspired this collection, and particularly to Anna Ticho, who opened her home to so many people—continuing to shape contemporary Israeli culture to this day. I admire Timna Seligman, Senior Curator of Ticho House, for her vision and friendship.

Among the many books I consulted during my research, I would particularly like to mention David Reifler's *Days of Ticho*; Irit Salmon's *Ticho House: A Jerusalem Landmark*; Timna Seligman's *Anna Ticho: Lifescape*; Betty Falkenberg's *Else Lasker-Schüler: A Life*; and Peter Cole's *Hebrew Writers on Writing*.

Thank you to my spouse, Rabbi Yonatan Sadoff, and to my children, Tiferet Tehilla, Maayan Tekhelet, Oz Lev, and Atara Zohara, for motivating me to write despite the challenges associated with pursuing a creative lifestyle in a foreign land, while raising four young children.

This book would not exist without Jessica Bell, Amie McCracken, Melanie Faith, Ashley Crantas, and Karen Jones at Vine Leaves Press, and their unwavering faith in this manuscript, as well as Linda Benjamin, Anna Plotkin, Jennifer Lang, and Dr. Lee Kofman, who guided me, with profound wisdom, through the intricacies of the book publishing agreement.

"Bride Immaculate" was published in the Energheia Italy Literary Prize Anthology—*i Racconti di Energheia* (September 2015): 89–103, as the winner of the 2014 Energheia Israel Literary Competition.

"Dancing in Splendor" was published in *Never Again: Remembering to Heal and Overcome*. Poetry and Stories from the Winners of the *Art of Unity Literary Award* (International Human Rights Art Movement Press, January 2025): 59–69.

"Degeneration" was published in *Parchment: A Journal of Contemporary Canadian Jewish Writing* 16 (2014): 98–118.

"Late Blossoms" was published in *Parchment: A Journal of Contemporary Canadian Jewish Writing* 16 (2014): 83–97.

"Representations of Jerusalem in the Poetry and Paintings of Else Lasker-Schüler" was published in *Gesher* 5
(November 2019): 57–60.

"Rose among the Thorns" was published in *Verge: Ritual,* edited
by Rebecca Bryson, Benjamin Jay and Giulia Mastrantoni
(Monash University Publishing, 2020): 84–91, and in the
Jewish Literary Journal (October 2023). It was a finalist in
the *Tiferet* literary journal's 2019 fiction contest.

Vine Leaves Press

Enjoyed this book?
Go to *vineleavespress.com* to find more.
Subscribe to our newsletter:

www.ingramcontent.com/pod-product-compliance
Lightning Source LLC
Chambersburg PA
CBHW010828250626
47169CB00010B/2991